"I'm not doing this job for you. I'm doing this for your staff."

"As long as the result is the same," he said in a low rumble. Despite the fog-chilled air, her skin heated as if it were noon on an August day.

If she moved her hand just a few inches, she would brush against the denim adorning his hard-muscled thighs. She had to create some distance somehow. "If I can be honest? Any marriage entered into under the conditions you describe is doomed to failure."

"I never fail."

"There's always a first time."

He leaned down until his warm breath caressed her cheek. "We'll see."

An answering warmth welled deep inside her, an insistent compulsion she needed to stop before she did something stupid.

Their gazes met. His was heavy, matching the heaviness between her legs. "I'm sorr—" she began.

He shook his head, once. Then his lips descended on hers, firm, hot, insistent.

Dear Reader,

A few years ago, I had dinner with a friend who is a corporate recruiter. Her expertise was finding the right candidate for specialized jobs that might be harder to fill than normal. As she was describing one of her most recent assignments, the proverbial light bulb went off over my head: What if a recruiter was asked not to find a work candidate, but a spouse?

Enter Luke Dallas. Business is a game he plays to win. When his employees' futures are threatened, Luke will do anything to save their jobs—including getting married. When he bumps into Danica Novak, an executive recruiter in urgent need of a salary, he thinks he's found the perfect solution. She'll recruit a wife for him. After all, isn't marriage just like business—a negotiation between two parties who have a mutual investment in a future outcome?

Just one problem: he forgot to add love into his calculations.

I am thrilled beyond words to be making my debut with Harlequin Desire. I had so much fun writing this book, and I hope you will enjoy reading Luke and Danica's story!

Happy reading!

Susannah

SUSANNAH ERWIN

———

WANTED: BILLIONAIRE'S WIFE

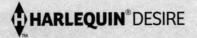

Recycling programs
for this product may
not exist in your area.

ISBN-13: 978-1-335-60366-1

Wanted: Billionaire's Wife

Copyright © 2019 by Susannah Erwin

All rights reserved. Except for use in any review, the reproduction or
utilization of this work in whole or in part in any form by any electronic,
mechanical or other means, now known or hereafter invented, including
xerography, photocopying and recording, or in any information storage
or retrieval system, is forbidden without the written permission of the
publisher, Harlequin Enterprises Limited, 22 Adelaide St. West, 40th Floor,
Toronto, ON M5H 4E3, Canada.

This is a work of fiction. Names, characters, places and incidents are
either the product of the author's imagination or are used fictitiously,
and any resemblance to actual persons, living or dead, business
establishments, events or locales is entirely coincidental.

This edition published by arrangement with Harlequin Books S.A.

For questions and comments about the quality of this book,
please contact us at CustomerService@Harlequin.com.

® and TM are trademarks of Harlequin Enterprises Limited or its
corporate affiliates. Trademarks indicated with ® are registered in the
United States Patent and Trademark Office, the Canadian Intellectual
Property Office and in other countries.

Printed in U.S.A.

A lover of storytelling in all forms, **Susannah Erwin** worked for major film studios before writing her first novel, which won RWA's Golden Heart® Award. She lives in Northern California with her husband and a very spoiled but utterly delightful cat.

Books by Susannah Erwin

Harlequin Desire

Wanted: Billionaire's Wife

Visit her Author Profile page at Harlequin.com, or susannaherwin.com, for more titles.

You can find Susannah Erwin on Facebook, along with other Harlequin Desire authors, at Facebook.com/harlequindesireauthors!

To Jeff, my very own happy-ever-after.

One

Danica Novak wanted a hot shower, cool bedsheets and at least ten hours of uninterrupted sleep after her early morning cross-country flight. Instead, she got a claim form for lost luggage, a taxi driver who hit every possible red light between the airport in San Francisco and her office building in Palo Alto, and yet another phone squabble with her parents' health insurance company about her brother's medical bills. This was the third person she'd talked to since her plane landed, and it wasn't yet 11:00 a.m. in California.

"The treatment isn't covered?" She braced her cell phone between her right shoulder and ear while using her hands to dig through her tote bag for any loose bills with which to pay the fare. Her credit card was useless, as she had discovered when she tried to buy food on the plane. Her sudden trip to Rhode Island at last-minute airfare prices had eaten up what remained of her cushion. "You can't negotiate to bring the costs down? At all?"

The driver stared at her through the rearview mirror, his fingers tapping an impatient rhythm on the steering wheel. When her eyes met his in the mirror, he flicked the meter back on. Danica smiled at him through gritted teeth and held up her index finger in the universal plea for just one more minute, while mustering the strength to keep her voice pitched at a pleasant conversational level.

She learned as a teenager, while helping her father apply for the license for his dry-cleaning business, that getting angry with faceless bureaucracies rarely resulted in a positive outcome. "Yes, I understand you've been told the treatment is classified as elective. Can I talk to a manager about this? Hello?" She stared at the phone. The call had dropped—or she had been hung up on.

A staccato beep from the car's horn ripped her attention back to the driver. "Lady, I gotta go."

"One second, please?" She put the phone down to better sift through the contents of her bag. The emergency twenty she always carried had to be somewhere—aha! She added it to the other bills and thrust the fare at the driver, scrambling out of the car as fast as the vinyl seat would let her. The taxi took off, the late Monday-morning sunshine bouncing off its fenders.

She stretched her neck, the bunched muscles in her shoulders protesting when she turned her head from side to side, and opened the glass door to the office building. It seemed a century ago when she last passed through the entrance, racing out in the middle of the day to pack for an emergency visit home. She was still reeling from the shock of seeing her brother, Matt, a perpetual motion machine since birth, so still in his hospital bed.

Matt had been a surprise baby, arriving eight years after Danica to the entire family's delight. Now a high-school senior, he'd attracted attention from universities for his athletic ability. Until two weeks ago, when a freak three-way collision during a football game caused a massive concussion, a fractured femur and spinal shock.

Now out of danger, his prognosis was good for a full recovery, but his doctors worried he wasn't responding as well as he could to conventional treatment. The experimental spinal therapy the insurance company was currently denying might speed up his return to health, but they wouldn't know unless a way was found to pay for it. And she'd find one. She'd told her parents she would take care of it, and she hadn't let them down yet.

Once inside, she closed her eyes and took a deep breath. Only four companies shared the office building, and the lobby was empty most times of day. She welcomed the quiet, letting it wash over her. Family leave was officially over. Time to switch back to worker bee. The Rinaldi Executive Search presentation to Ruby Hawk Technologies was in two days, and it needed to be perfect. Her promised promotion from Johanna Rinaldi's assistant to search consultant depended on it. She grabbed a free copy of the *Silicon Valley Weekly off the lobby's reception desk*, hoping to catch up on the latest tech-industry news while she headed down the corridor to the Rinaldi offices. The tabloid newspaper was accessible online, but the print version was easier to read while walking. As if the universe had decided she needed a reminder of just how crucial the next few days would be, a color photo of Luke Dallas, the thirty-three-year-old CEO and founder of Ruby Hawk Technologies, stared out at her from the front page.

Like most people in the valley, Danica followed the meteoric rise of Ruby Hawk Technologies with awe. But the man behind the company held a special fascination for her. She long thought Luke Dallas looked as if he should be brooding on a windswept English moor rather than writing code in a glass-and-steel California office. His strong, chiseled features were a perfect match for the rumors of his hard-nosed tactics. In a town that tolerated eccentric if driven geniuses, he stood out for his demanding demeanor.

A shiver traced her spine as her gaze met his in the photo, the blue of his eyes stunning even in newsprint. She would soon be sitting across the table from that stare. A month ago, Danica discovered Ruby Hawk had terminated their contract with their search agency. She knew Johanna and Luke had gone to business school together, and she'd used that information to land a meeting to pitch Ruby Hawk their services. He was scheduled to sit in that meeting.

Surely, he couldn't be that arresting in real life. It must be a trick of the photographer's, maybe the light—

Her peripheral vision screamed out a warning just in

time. She barely avoided colliding with a very broad, very muscular male chest. She swallowed her gasp of appreciation for the obviously fine physique under the tailored button-down shirt, threw the man a quick smile of apology and returned to perusing the article while she rummaged in her bag for her office key.

It took a second before the man's face fully registered. She looked up from the newspaper and stared at him. Then she glanced down at the photo. Then back at the man. Her mouth went dry as her heartbeat thudded in her ears.

Luke Dallas stood in front of the closed door of Rinaldi Executive Search. In the flesh. All six feet, four inches of him, from his wavy dark hair to his rather impressively sized loafers.

She'd been wrong. He was indeed that arresting—and more—in person. A two-dimensional image was incapable of capturing the aura of danger in his stance, coiled tension threatening to spring into action at the slightest provocation. The photo revealed the handsome symmetry of his features, but couldn't impart the sheer sensuality and command. This was a man who got what he wanted and didn't care how. Pinned by the force of his gaze, she shivered as his expression darkened. The air grew heavy, thickening with the ominous atmosphere of two weather fronts about to collide into a supercell.

She was in the direct path of the storm.

This should have been a day for triumph. Instead, Luke Dallas's jaw hurt from hours of clenching his teeth. It was a new sensation. He was always in control, no matter the situation.

But that was before this morning. Before a casual meeting in an out-of-the-way coffee shop, away from prying eyes and ears, to sign the deal memo for his company's acquisition turned into an ambush orchestrated by Irene Stavros and her father, Nestor. His vision still flashed red.

He'd travelled straight from the meeting, the ultimatum handed to him by Nestor running on a constant loop, to Johanna Rinaldi's boutique search firm. Johanna was the only person he could think of under the time-crunched circumstances who could help to extricate him from the trap Nestor had pulled closed so artfully.

Where the hell was she? Her office was locked tight and no one answered the door or the phone. His patience had just stretched past its breaking point when a woman, who couldn't be bothered to look where she was going, nearly ran him over. She stared at him with eyes so wide they threatened to take over the rest of her face. Pretty eyes though. Big and green. A man could get lost in those depths if he wasn't careful.

Then she blinked, breaking the connection, and his anger came back.

"Can I help you?" he barked, partially to cover being caught staring at a stranger, no matter how attractive, and partially because she wasn't Johanna and, right now, Johanna was the only person he wanted to see.

"You're Luke Dallas." Her gaze ping-ponged between the newspaper clutched in her hand and his face. "But our meeting isn't until Wednesday."

"You work for Johanna?" Finally. Maybe his day could get back on track and he could salvage what was left of it.

"Um." Her eyes were still wide as she ran a hand through her messy blond ponytail, then used it to tug on a white shirt that looked like it had been put on straight off the floor. Finally, she held it out to be shaken. "Yes. I do. I'm Danica. Novak. Danica Novak."

He shook her proffered hand. When he pressed against it, her fingers trembled and she leaned back, as if she were Little Red Riding Hood and he the Big Bad Wolf and they were standing in Grandmother's house. An appealing rosy shade appeared on her high cheekbones.

"It seems you know my name."

"Yes, well," she said, waving the newspaper clutched in her left hand, "it helps to have a visual aid." She gave him a tentative smile, and if he thought her eyes pretty before, the smile turned them downright stunning. Then the newspaper headline caught his gaze and made him forget any nonsense about the eyes being the windows to the soul.

"May I see that?" he asked. She handed it over.

He read the article, the hallway walls pressing in further with every word. The *Weekly*'s business reporter Cinco Jackson somehow had received wind of Luke's talks with the Stavros Group, despite his best efforts to keep them quiet. The article outlined the rumors surrounding the acquisition, calling it a done deal with the papers due to be signed imminently. Luke would be lucky to make it ten feet past Ruby Hawk's front door without his employees questioning him about timing and next steps.

Thanks to his family, plus some savvy investments of his own, Luke could've retired after college graduation and still lived an extremely comfortable life. But that was due to being born to the right parents. He hadn't earned it.

He refused to be like his stepsiblings, living off the fat of their inheritances. He wanted to build something, like his great-grandfather had. He wanted it to last, *unlike* his great-grandfather's legacy. The Draper & Dallas department store chain was long gone. The advancements made by Ruby Hawk in biofeedback and neural technology, however, could make lives better for generations.

He crushed the newspaper in his hand. Ruby Hawk Technologies was *his*. He'd created the company, pouring his own money into it. Now he needed additional capital for the company to reach its full potential, to prove to those who wrote him off as a rich dilettante that he had what it took to be a tech visionary.

He'd explored options for raising more money but none provided the combination of financing, ownership control and corporate independence Luke sought. Then Irene Stavros suggested he talk to her father. A month ago, Luke received a deal term sheet from Nestor.

On paper, it was perfect. The Stavros Group would buy Ruby Hawk and infuse the company with the cash it needed to expand, while allowing Ruby Hawk to continue to operate autonomously. The original management team, including Luke as CEO, would remain intact and he would continue to call all the shots without interference from the acquiring parent company. Anticipating an easy close to the deal, Luke ordered and installed expensive new equipment for his engineers. Then when he went to meet Nestor to sign the paperwork, Nestor revealed his trap. Unless Luke went along with Nestor's demands, he wouldn't have the means to make payroll in six months' time.

And now, the article. Thanks to it revealing the deal terms, his employees would be expecting their stock options to be worth millions upon the completion of the acquisition.

He had to save this deal. "Where's your boss?"

Her green eyes widened at the snap of his words.

"I've been here for half an hour and no one has answered the door or the phone. What kind of a business is this?" He thrust the tabloid back at her. He'd deal with the story later.

"We're very good at what we do. I'm sure there's an explanation." She shook out the crumpled paper.

He raised an eyebrow and looked at his watch.

Color rose even higher in her cheeks. "I just got off a plane. Johanna probably has a meeting off-site." She opened a substantial tote bag and searched inside. "Although that doesn't explain why Britt isn't on phone duty," she murmured under her breath. Her hand surfaced holding a key ring. "Wait here while I make sure the lights are on."

She swung open the door and disappeared inside,

shutting it behind her. He heard a stifled exclamation, followed by a loud thud. Just as he was about to investigate the noise, she emerged, slamming the door shut and leaning against it.

Her face made her white shirt seem dark gray by comparison. "Um, maybe you should wait at the diner next door. The coffee is good. It's all single origin, hand poured—"

"No." It would be a long time before he'd be able to drink coffee without the memory of that morning's meeting poisoning the taste. "What's wrong? Is someone hurt?"

She shook her head, her chest rapidly rising and falling.

"I'm going in." He gently took her hand off the doorknob. It trembled in his grasp.

Her chin snapped up. "No, please don't—"

He ignored her protestations. Was it a break-in? Vandalism? Or hungover coworkers, and she didn't want a prospective client to see what really went on at Rinaldi Executive Search?

The last thing he'd expected to see was emptiness. As in, not only were employees not at their desks, but the desks were gone too. The blinds were open and the sunshine revealed a reception area, barren save for a broken desk stool, naked metal shelves and scuffmarks on the bamboo laminate floors marking where furniture once stood. One lonely high-walled cubicle stood outside a door that led to an inner office empty of all furnishings.

"I thought maybe we were robbed." Danica stood

behind him in the doorway, her arms protectively hugging her chest. "But…"

He shook his head. Thieves would have left a mess. "This is the work of professional movers."

The hot fist in his stomach began to squeeze again. Johanna's disappearance was total. How could he so badly miscalculate twice in the same day?

"I was gone two weeks." Danica's voice was thin. "Two weeks." Her gaze, wild and unfocused, travelled around the empty space. She shuffled into the office like a sleepwalker who couldn't wake up. Her tote bag lay in her path, its contents scattered across the floor. Before he could clear it out of her way, her foot tangled in the thick strap.

He lunged, grasping her shoulders to keep her upright. This close, her hair consisted of a thousand shades of gold, from honey chestnut to palest yellow. Faint freckles dusted the pale skin stretched over a small, pointed nose. Her lips were softly curved, the bottom lip presenting the perfect amount of plumpness. Vanilla spiked with cinnamon teased his nose. For a second, he was tempted to see if she tasted just as spicy sweet.

Then reality landed a roundhouse to his gut.

His plan for saving Ruby Hawk had disappeared with the office furnishings that used to grace the Rinaldi office.

"Thank you for the save." Danica heard her voice as if it came from a long distance. Maybe she fell asleep on the plane, and this was just a bad nightmare brought on by the pressure of finishing the pitch presentation? But despite the number of blinks, the vision in front of her stayed the same.

Luke Dallas, CEO of Ruby Hawk Technologies. A *Doctor Who* fan had confided in her that Luke was called Luke Dalek behind his back, because he never met a human emotion he didn't try to exterminate.

Luke Dallas, who had very firm muscles under his Silicon Valley uniform of blue button-down shirt paired with khakis. Underneath his clothes, he must put a Greek god to shame. She grasped the silky cotton of his shirt, his biceps flexing under her fingers. He even smelled like she imagined a Greek god would: like the outdoors after a rainstorm over a base of expensive leather and fresh citrus. The room began to spin, faster and faster, and she closed her eyes.

"Breathe," he said. "In and out."

She did as he commanded, allowing herself to lean into him, just a little, craving the intense sense of confidence and security his arms provided. Then he abruptly let go. Her eyes flew open.

"I don't have time to take you to urgent care if you fall and hurt yourself." His jaw clenched as his gaze travelled the barren suite. "I have to leave."

Think, Danica, think fast. But her mind was a jumble of scattershot fragments mixed with bursts of pure panic. All she knew was if he left, he would take with him the chance of pitching Rinaldi Executive Search's services to him. And with that would go her promised promotion.

She needed to find her boss. This had to be a huge misunderstanding.

"Johanna must have moved offices while I was gone. I was a bit hard to reach." It was the truth. Matt's hospital floor didn't allow cell phones. "Let me call her."

She picked up her treacherous tote bag and scooped the fallen items back into it. Where was her phone? She knew she got off the plane with it. She had it in the taxi—

Oh, no. She placed it on the taxi's back seat while searching for the fare. And she never picked it back up. It could be anywhere from Marin to Monterey.

"Something else wrong?" His hard stare caused her skin to prickle.

"Nothing is wrong. I forgot something, that's all," she said, keeping her tone pleasant. It was if he could see through her and wasn't impressed. Just like in high school, when the kids at the top of the social pyramid made sure she knew she would never ascend to their heights.

He folded his arms. "Seems to me a lot is wrong. Starting with the empty office."

"I'm going to my desk to straighten this out. Will you give me fifteen minutes?" Please, she prayed, let there be a working office phone on the premises. And please let Johanna have an amazing explanation that didn't defy logic.

He nodded. She held her head high until she was behind her cubicle walls, out of his view. Then her shoulders crumbled.

Her cubicle was empty of everything but a file box.

The lid was off, and inside were the few personal items she kept in the space. On top were the comic-book action figures that used to decorate her shelves. They had been a gag gift from her brother when she moved to California, a reminder she was stronger than she looked.

Her nose stung. She willed the tears away. Crying only caused more problems, a lesson she had learned well.

A note was taped to the outside of the box, the cream-colored envelope embossed with Johanna's initials. The heavy, linen-weave paper was leaden in her hands.

Hey, Danica!
I didn't want to disturb you while you were with your family. But the Stavros Group offered me an amazing opportunity! I'm their new head of Asia-Pacific talent recruitment. I'll be based in Sydney and traveling all over the world. They needed me right away so I couldn't wait until you came back. :-(

Britt already has a new job, yay! Speaking of, do me a favor and make sure Britt forwarded the phones to the answering service? ;-)

I'll try to call you when I get settled, but I'll be super busy so it might be a while. Here's your final paycheck and the number for the lawyer in charge of the business dissolution in case you have questions.
Ciao!
Johanna xoxo

Danica pulled out the attached pay slip. Two weeks' severance had been added to it. Two weeks. That was all she was worth to Johanna? After giving her three years of her life, helping her build the company from the ground up, never taking vacation and only the very rare sick day? The emergency family leave had been the first time she'd been away from the office for more than forty-eight hours in a row.

She sank to the floor. This was worse than when her ex-boyfriend left her. At least then she'd had a job and could contribute to the family finances. Now? She didn't even have her beaten-up car. She'd asked her roommate, Mai, to sell it for her to cover her share of the household expenses, since her plane ticket had eaten up her meager bank account. Nor could she ask Mai to let her slide on her rent payment. Mai's finances were almost as precarious as hers.

Danica always managed to find the glimmer of light in darkness, to think her way out of what seemed like insurmountable odds. Until now. Try as hard as she could, her mind remained an opaque blank.

Luke watched Danica march to her cubicle, ponytail swinging as if she didn't have a care in the world. He couldn't help but notice other rounder portions of her anatomy also swaying. Too bad she was lying about reaching Johanna. He'd tried calling her several times himself. No answer, only voice mail.

He should return to his office and come up with plans B through Z. He would just have to sidestep his team's questions about the acquisition the best he could.

A sniffle-like sound echoed through the empty suite. He shook his head. Tears were a cheap, manipulative trick. He reached for the doorknob.

A second sniffle ricocheted through the air, followed by a third.

Damn it. He turned and walked to the cubicle.

The noises were Danica shredding what looked like expensive stationery into tiny pieces of confetti. "Wanton destruction. Effective," he said.

She gave him a quick smile, her eyes suspiciously bright, before returning to her task. "Johanna moved to Sydney."

He couldn't keep the surprise out of his voice. "You got her on the phone?"

She shook her head. "She left an old-fashioned note. I'd show you but it's not legible now." More paper fragments fell from her hands. "I guess the meeting on Wednesday is cancelled."

"Yes." A strange twinge of something like regret hit him at the thought of never seeing her again, but he shook it off. "I'm leaving. Good luck." He held out his hand to be shaken.

She took it. Her palm fit against his as if it was meant to be there.

He cleared his throat. "If you hear from Johanna, tell her I need—"

His gaze fixated on a scrap of paper near his shoe. *Stavr* was written on it in loopy cursive letters. "Why is Johanna in Sydney?"

Danica shrugged. "Her note said she got her dream job." She kicked at the scraps.

"A job with whom?" His stomach muscles contracted as if anticipating a hard blow.

"The Stavros Group. Why?"

The blow landed, square in his gut. He now saw just how thoroughly Nestor and Irene had prepared the trap. He couldn't help but wonder who else in his social circle they'd co-opted. He bet if he called Gwen, the last woman he dated, he'd find she was filming out of the country—for one of the Stavros Group's production companies.

And he'd walked into it like a green MBA just out of business school, all theoretical book learning with none of the street smarts he had honed over the years. His fists bunched, nails digging sharply into his skin. It was either that or punch the wall, and the cubicle looked like one good blow would topple it over. "I can't believe I didn't see this," he ground out.

Danica stopped tearing paper, her gaze fixing on his. "What does Johanna's new job have to do with you?"

He shook his head, the bile closing his throat and bottling his words deep inside. Nestor and Irene were three steps ahead of him, always had been. They took Johanna off the game board, knowing she would be his first move. It was predictable, he had to admit. He and Irene and Johanna had been at business school together. Irene knew his social circle almost as well as he did. Damn it.

He strode out of the cubicle. "I have to get back to my office."

"Oh, no, you don't." Danica beat him to the outer

door and stood in his way. "You're not leaving until you tell me what is going on."

He ignored her, veering right.

She dodged him with a grace he hadn't seen since the last time he was dragged to a benefit for the San Francisco Ballet. She set her feet and held her arms out to block his passage. He couldn't help but notice how her stance caused her shirt buttons to strain against her full breasts, creating shadowy gaps that tempted further exploration.

He dragged his gaze away and reached for the doorknob. "I don't have time for this game."

Her hand grabbed his wrist, her fingers landing on his pulse point. Their gazes met, clashed in a lightning strike that sent electricity crackling through the air.

Her chin dropped, and she looked up at him from under dark gold eyelashes. The tip of her pink tongue darted out to wet her plump lips, her breaths coming faster. Her remarkable eyes almost glowed in the dust-filled light. What if he leaned in, like so—

Before he could put his thoughts into action, she snapped her head up. The static in the atmosphere dissipated. She let his wrist go but he could feel the pressure of her fingers on his skin.

"This is not a game. This is my life." Her voice cracked on the last word, and she took a deep breath. "Before today, I had a job I loved in executive recruitment. I was really good at it too. My title might have been assistant, but I made most of the placements and I was finally about to be promoted. But this morning, poof!" She snapped her fingers. "And judging by your behavior, you're connected to the magic trick that made my job disappear. You owe me an explanation."

He couldn't tell her the truth. No one got the better of him. Especially not Irene and her father.

Then Danica's words clicked. *Executive recruitment.* She was also a recruiter.

It wasn't the most elegant solution. She'd think him irrational, to start, and maybe he was. He certainly wasn't acting like himself, leaning in to kiss a stranger just because he found her mouth intriguing.

Yet when he ran a split-second mental check of the pros and cons, it made sense. In fact, it might work better than his initial plan, which had required Johanna's unpredictable cooperation.

Danica's words made it sound like her entire world had imploded. She needed him. Or rather, he corrected himself, she needed his offer of employment. It was always beneficial to have the upper hand in a business relationship.

Yes, he found her attractive. But his discipline, at both work and play, was legendary. "You say you're good at executive recruitment?"

"The best." Her expression turned wary. "Why do you ask?"

"Because I need a wife ASAP. And you're going to recruit one for me."

Two

"You need a *wife*?" Danica was surprised her legs still held her up. "And you want me to *recruit* one for you?"

It didn't make sense. Luke Dallas should have no trouble finding a wife. His effect on women was well documented. She herself spent only three minutes in his presence before she started tripping over her bag. If she hadn't managed to break the spell his nearness cast over her, she would have thrown all professionalism to the wind and kissed him. And then prayed for an earthquake to swallow her as she'd be the laughing stock of Silicon Valley: the assistant who threw herself at Luke Dallas. Johanna *especially* would—

The shoe dropped, hard.

"Is that why you're here?" Danica stared at Luke. "You were going to ask Johanna to do this."

A ruddy glint appeared on his sun-bronzed cheekbones. "Do you want a job or not?"

She managed to corral her thoughts into something resembling coherency. "I don't know the first thing about finding wives. Vice-presidents of finance? Yes. Lifetime partners? You're on your own."

"What's the difference?" he countered. "I give you my list of requirements. You find candidates who match those requirements."

"But," she sputtered, searching for words to make him understand, "a wife isn't an employee. What about, oh, I don't know, compatibility? Life goals?"

"I look for employees who are compatible with my company's culture and share my goals for its future. I expect the same from a wife." He sounded as if he were ordering a custom car, instead of entering a committed relationship with a human being.

"But you can fire an employee. You can't fire a wife!"

"It's called divorce. Look, I hire employees who are the best of the best. But I don't comb the world looking for them. I hire someone to do that for me." He leaned into the door, his broad shoulder just scant inches from where hers rested against the polished wooden surface.

Her pulse doubled. It had to be from outrage at his ridiculous request. It certainly wasn't caused by having his attention laser focused on her, his gaze demanding she meet his. "I'd be thrilled to be an executive recruiter for you, but—"

"It's the same principle. I don't have time for the necessary getting-to-know-you dates to ensure a potential spouse fits my specific requirements. I'm hiring you to do the vetting for me. Simple."

"Only it's not—"

"The successful candidate will need to sign a prenuptial contract so that I can, indeed, 'fire' her without consequences if necessary. Just like an employment contract, which you and I will have. It's highly reasonable." His direct gaze dared her to disagree.

No wonder he earned the nickname Luke Dalek. He made marriage sound like lines of binary code. "What about falling in love?"

He raised an eyebrow, like a teacher silently reprimanding a student for failing to add two plus two correctly. "The successful candidate will be well compensated for meeting my requirements. As will you for conducting the search. I assume three hundred thousand dollars will cover your retainer fee and costs."

"That doesn't answer my—wait. Three hundred thousand dollars?" At his nod, blood thudded in her ears. This time, his nearness had nothing to do with it.

Three. Hundred. *Thousand.* Dollars. What remained of the bills for Matt's surgery could be paid outright and he could start the experimental treatment. Her parents could stop worrying. Her rent payments would be covered, staving off homelessness for the foreseeable future.

There was even enough money to start her own

search firm. Never again rely on an employer's empty promises.

It sounded too good to be true. And in her experience, when things sounded too good to be true, it meant they would end only in tears: hers. "There are lots of people who are professional matchmakers. Like that TV show, *Matchmaker for Millionaires*, or whatever it's called. Why not go to her?"

His upper lip curled. "I would rather replace my laptop with a typewriter. I told you, I don't have time for the conventional courtship a matchmaker would require. I'm hiring you because my criteria include a successful business track record, experience with high-level philanthropy and an elite education. Qualities you should be familiar with in executive recruitment."

"Seems like a rather extreme way to meet women." Exhaustion always caused her mouth to operate separately from her brain's tact center.

His gaze narrowed, then his mouth upturned ever so slightly. He leaned closer to her. "If I just needed to meet women, I wouldn't require your services. Believe me." His low tones rumbled in her ear, causing her knees to turn to water.

She braced herself against the wall. She didn't want to find Luke Dallas desirable. He was easy to look at, sure. His muscles belonged on a museum statue. His eyes could be used as interrogation weapons: one deep gaze into those blue pools and she was sure spies of all genders would be happy to spill their secrets. It was fun following his exploits in the gossip columns from afar—okay, exciting to imagine herself in the designer dresses of his dates. But in person? Intimidating. Arrogant. And asking the impossible.

Too late, she realized Luke continued to speak. She tuned in just in time to hear him say, "If you complete the search in one month, you'll earn a fifty-thousand-dollar bonus."

"Fifty...thousand..." The room began to spin around her once more.

"Breathe," he said. He put a hand on her upper arm to keep her steady. Sparks flew from where he touched her, crackling through her nervous system. "You should work on that."

It was a lot of money. Money her family needed. She searched his gaze, looking for a catch. She saw only determination.

"Well?" He looked at his smartwatch. "The offer is off the table in three minutes."

Finding suitable contenders shouldn't be a problem if she focused on education and work history. Charity work and social affiliations would also help her determine if they met his criteria. Thankfully, she had backed up the firm's database of recruitment targets before she took her family leave. Johanna rarely changed her own email passwords, much less the password to the cloud storage site Danica used for the firm's important files, so access to the information shouldn't be a problem.

The ethics of finding him a bride, however... She bit her lower lip. But he was right. Executive search hinged on making a successful match between the employer and the candidate. What he wanted wasn't too much of a leap. She blurted out the next thing that popped into her head. "I'm not asking about sexual histories. That's all on you."

A swift grin transformed his face. It made him seem approachable, even charming. "Does that mean you accept the job?"

"I have a few conditions." Her voice echoed in the empty office. "I'll find you three women who fit your criteria. However, getting one of them to agree to marry you is your job. And if no one puts on your ring, I still get paid."

"Only three?"

She held up her hand and checked off items on her fingers as she spoke. "You're asking me to identify suitable candidates, investigate their backgrounds, check their references and ascertain their interest in the potential—" she was going to say *position* but changed her mind "—opening."

He raised an eyebrow and gave her a devastating smirk. Too late, she realized the word she chose was almost as suggestive as the one she discarded. "In one month. Three feasible choices are a very healthy outcome," she said, managing to continue.

"Fine. I accept. But I must agree each one satisfies my requirements before I sign off on the completion of your contract." A gleam lit his gaze when he stressed the word *satisfies*.

"You agree they fulfill the requirements on paper before you meet them. Any satisfaction that occurs after is up to you." She bit her lower lip to stop from returning his smirk.

His gaze lingered on her mouth. If he was trying to fluster her, he was doing a good job. She folded her arms and lifted her chin.

That unholy glint of laughter remained in his gaze. "And your other conditions?"

She resisted the urge to wipe her damp palms on her trousers. "An office to work in, a corporate cell phone and an open expense account. Oh, and health insurance. Starting today." She kept her gaze steadily on his through sheer force of will. He really did have the most amazing eyes. Deep blue with flecks of gray—or were they deep gray with flecks of blue? Either way, they reminded her of pictures she had seen of ancient Roman mosaics in her parents' home city of Zagreb, the colors deep and rich and playing off each other.

This time an actual smile dented one side of his face. "Come by Ruby Hawk after lunch and I'll have someone set you up with a workspace, phone, benefits and credit card."

Danica exhaled. It felt good to have her lungs back in working order. "It's a deal."

"Not yet. I have conditions of my own. One, this is confidential."

She narrowed her gaze. "Searches usually are."

"Two, you'll sign a nondisclosure agreement. No talking to the press, your relatives or your partner." He raised an eyebrow. "I assume you have one."

"I never talk to the press. I keep my work and private life separate."

"And the partner?"

"None of your business, but not an issue." Was that

a flash in his gaze? Not that it was any concern of hers. Yes, he was attractive, but so had been her ex. Who dumped her to marry a woman who sounded a lot like Luke's ideal candidate.

He nodded. "We'll tell the staff at Ruby Hawk you're a consultant working on a research project for me. And three, while I understand asking certain questions are not in your job description—" he paused and his one-sided smile deepened "—your candidates must be single and free of romantic entanglements."

His phone rang, an insistent buzz. He looked at it, and the CEO feared across Silicon Valley reappeared. "I have to take this. I'll see you in my office at two thirty." It was a command, not a question. Before she could respond, he was gone, leaving eddies in the air.

She let out her breath as the adrenaline surging in his presence slowly retreated. Her gaze swept the bare walls and scuffed floors. It was hard to believe two weeks ago she thought her job was secure. Of course, two weeks ago she also thought her strong, athletic teenage brother would remain in the best of health. Before the accident, Danica thought her life was on a straight road, with maybe the occasional dip or hill. Now? Nothing but blind curves and unmarked hazards.

Like the blind curve Luke Dallas represented. She squeezed her eyes shut. She'd make it work. To help her brother get the care he needed, she'd do almost anything.

She left the office with her box of personal possessions in hand and headed to the nearest library to log into the employee-only portal on the Rinaldi Execu-

tive Search website. As she anticipated, the passwords
hadn't been changed. She filled out the template agreement for executive search services, changing the words
and terms as necessary. After her finger hovered over
the keyboard for several heartbeats, she pressed Send.

Luke wasn't sure if he'd made an expensive blun-
der or hit upon a stroke of genius. The decision to hire
Danica Novak to find him a wife so he could jump
through Nestor Stavros's ridiculous hoop seemed right
at the time. A week later, driving in his car on his way
to work, it seemed like a damn foolish idea. Especially
since he had yet to see any viable work product from
Ms. Novak.

He refused to think he been taken in by big green
eyes and a luscious mouth meant to be kissed slowly
and thoroughly. He found her physically attractive, yes.
But she also exhibited a quick wit and a willingness to
go toe to toe with him that suggested she was intelli-
gent and more than capable. He just needed to see the
evidence of it. Now.

He parked his BMW i8 in the parking space marked
with his name and strode through the glass doors engraved with the Ruby Hawk logo, forgoing the elevator
in favor of taking the stairs two by two up to the third
floor that housed the main operations. Today was going
to be yet another difficult one. Cinco Jackson wrote
another article about the Stavros Group acquisition,
and this time he mentioned the deal might fall apart if
certain unnamed conditions weren't met.

Anjuli Patel met him as he exited the stairwell. He

did a double take as he took in her outfit. The chief financial officer of Ruby Hawk and his second-in-command, she normally wore carefully color-coordinated outfits and tasteful jewelry. This morning she looked as if one of her three-year-old twins had chosen her clothing. "Another article just appeared in the *Silicon Valley Weekly*," she said. "My husband texted me from the gym at 6:00 a.m."

"Yes. I saw it. I'm sure everyone has," he answered without breaking stride.

Anjuli fell in beside him and matched his speed. "How much truth is in it? Is the Stavros Group removing you when the deal goes through? *Is* the deal going through?" Her dark gaze sparked with anxious curiosity. She knew as well as he did how much the influx of cash from the acquisition was vitally needed.

"Let's talk." He beelined for his office. Like most tech companies, Ruby Hawk employees worked in an open plan bullpen. No doors, no cubicles, just desks pushed together to form team clusters. But recently Luke took over one of the glass-walled conference rooms that ringed the outer wall for more privacy during the acquisition discussions. He'd need it today.

"Let's talk in a good way? Or let's talk and it's bad?" she asked.

"Just be prepared," he said. "Run the numbers if the Stavros Group stays with the deal, and then run the numbers if they don't."

"Which set do you want first?"

The sooner he knew what he was up against, the better. "The latter."

"So it's bad." Her worried gaze swept over the engineers sitting at low desks. A few browser windows featuring the *Silicon Valley Weekly* website closed as Luke and Anjuli passed by.

"It might be." He increased his stride to pull ahead of her.

His steps slowed as he neared the door to the conference room. A clump of his top executives occupied the space between him and the door. Every single person standing outside his office he had handpicked to be on his team. In many cases, he persuaded them to leave lucrative salaries and promising career trajectories to join him at Ruby Hawk. He owed them, more than he could express.

"There he is." The knot of executives pressed forward.

"Is it true?"

"What's happening with the acquisition?"

"Are you leaving the company?"

He caught sight of a messy blond ponytail on the outer fringes of the group. Good. He needed Danica—or rather, he corrected his thoughts grimly, he needed her work, now more than ever.

He held up a hand and the questions quieted down. "Don't pay attention to the rumors. Our response is to keep our heads down and continue to do good work. But I do need to see her." He indicated with a jerk of his chin for Danica to come forward.

Her startled gaze met his. "Me?" she sputtered.

"You. Anjuli, let's meet after you run those numbers. Everyone else, back to your desks. If you want to gossip, do it on your own time." He stepped forward to usher Danica into his office as the small crowd dispersed at his command.

Danica didn't have time to form a protest. His hand on the small of her back guided her, its warmth radiating through the thin cotton jersey of her shirt. He indicated a chair in front of his desk and let go of her arm, not a second too soon for her comfort. The door shut behind them with a resounding click.

"What can I do for you?" she asked, sitting gingerly on the edge of a clear molded acrylic chair. Her back was to the glass wall, but her spine prickled with the heat of at least half a dozen stares aimed straight at her.

He sat down on the opposite side of the repurposed-wood conference table. He pushed a button on a remote control and mechanized shades unrolled over the windows, shielding them from the curious gazes.

The light in the room dimmed, the atmosphere changing from corporate to intimate. She was very aware they were the only two people in the room.

His shoulders seemed to fall slightly. It was a small chink in his usually impenetrable armor of arrogant self-confidence. She yearned to reach out and smooth the faint creases marring his brow. "What's wrong?" she tried again, her tone soft.

The vulnerability disappeared as quickly as it had revealed itself, causing the temperature in the room to fall a few degrees. "Nothing I can't handle."

She resisted the urge to turn around and point at

the now-shaded glass wall. "The angry mob searching for pitchforks and torches was just my imagination?"

His eyebrows drew together. "A vivid one. That was nowhere near a mob, and they weren't angry."

"A group of concerned employees, then. Is it the article about the Stavros Group pulling out of the deal?"

"I need your candidate list."

It was a good thing she was already sitting. The shock would have blown her off her feet. "I sent you my preliminary list days ago. That's why I was standing there, hoping to catch you for your reaction." She pulled an email printout from the folder she carried and placed it on his desk.

He glanced down at the paper, and then his head came up sharply. "I thought this was a list of rejected candidates. I deleted it." He pushed it aside. "It's been five working days. I need your results. Now."

He deleted her hard work? Without so much as an acknowledgment he had received it? "I know it's been five days!" she shot back. "Five days of you ignoring my emails, my phone calls, my chat invitations, my texts." How dare he put this on her? "I did everything but parade naked in front of that window to get your attention!"

The light in his eyes changed. Prickles formed on her skin. "I answer communications when I have something to say. No answer from me means 'No.'" A corner of his mouth turned up in a smirk. "Although no one's tried parading naked before."

That treacherous heat suffused her cheeks again. "If this is the way you treat your employees' attempts to get in touch with you, no wonder they talk as if the company needs to be measured for a coffin behind your back."

His lips compressed into a thin line. "They do no such thing."

"I know this room resembles a bubble, but that's no excuse for talking like you live in one." Luke was powerful and wealthy. Perhaps his lofty status kept him from seeing the ground below him. "I'm practically locked up in a converted supply closet because you don't want anyone to know why I'm here, and even *I* know the acquisition is in trouble. You need to talk to your employees. Starting with me."

His gaze was the glacial blue of an iceberg beneath the surface and just as dangerous. "Fine. Let's talk. If you're having difficulty performing the task assigned to you, we should rethink this arrangement."

What? Her breath came in staccato bursts. She'd told her parents she would pay for Matt's treatment. She refused to let that become a lie. "I performed the task assigned to me. That list is the result of hours of impeccable research. Every single person has been vetted and meets your criteria." She returned his arctic gaze with a heated glare. "How dare you delete it?"

He stood up, his broad, muscled form towering over her. "You submitted a list of women already known to me. Therefore, it's unusable."

She sprang to her feet. He would not intimidate her with his stance. The top of her head came up to his Adam's apple, forcing her to tilt her head back so she could meet his gaze straight on. "It may be hard to be-

lieve, but every date you've ever had is not on a gossip
website. That is why I sent the list to you to vet. I need
your feedback." She leaned over and pointed at the
printout, her index finger planted firmly on his desk.

He raised a dismissive eyebrow and slid the paper
from underneath her finger, crumpling it up and tossing
it in a perfect arc into a nearby wastebasket. He then
put his hands on the desk and angled his torso over the
table. Scant inches separated them.

"The women on your list work in tech. You think
I'm not aware of talented up-and-coming executives?
I don't need you to tell me who I know and already
considered. I need you to find someone I *haven't* considered."

Danica huffed. "Remember what I said about communication? This would've been useful information to
have. A week ago."

He leaned even closer. The scent of expensive
leather and fresh citrus teased her nose. She got the
distinct sense of a tiger playing with his prey. The prey
might think it could escape. But the tiger was coiled to
jump and tear out the prey's throat in a blink.

"You're the search expert, not me," he said in a low,
controlled voice. "But common sense dictates looking
further afield than the client is able to do on his own
is a prerequisite for the job."

"You—" she began.

Then she stopped and considered his words.

He was right.

She had overlooked a basic step in conducting a
search: assess which candidates had already been re-

jected before she came on board. And yes, he could have explained the problem with her list in a timelier, if not infinitely more tactful, manner. But if he had, he wouldn't be Luke Dallas.

Her gaze fell. His shirt was open at the collar, revealing a triangle of sun-bronzed skin. A pulse leaped at the side of his neck, and for a split second she wanted to rest her lips there and see if he tasted as good as he smelled.

"You…" she started again. "You're right. I'm sorry. If you still want me to work on the search, I'll compile a better list." She snuck a glance at him from under her eyelashes. She expected chilly disdain, but there was something warm and contemplative deep in his eyes. A hot spark kindled in her chest as their gazes tangled.

"I only hire people who perform well at their tasks. You're still on the search. But I expect better results." He sat back down in his chair, taking his appealing scent with him. She stifled her disappointment.

"And you will get them. I promise." She turned to leave the room.

"Have dinner with me."

"What?" She whirled around so quickly she nearly caused self-induced whiplash.

He put down his tablet and looked up at her, leaning back in his seat. "I haven't given this project the specialized attention it needs. It's clear you don't have the necessary inputs to make correct assessments. I don't have time to remedy that right now. But I do have to eat later, so you might as well eat with me."

His words doused the spark's last flickers. "When you put it that way, how can I refuse?"

"I'll text you the address. I trust going into the city isn't a problem for you?" His tone made it clear it was a rhetorical question.

San Francisco was almost an hour each way on Caltrain, depending on the train schedules, and her exhausted brain was already looking forward to putting on pajamas and binging on reality TV with her roommate, Mai. She gave him her best, if forced, smile. "No. Not a problem."

"Good. I have a commitment beforehand, so I'll meet you there." His attention returned to his tablet and he became absorbed in whatever he was reading. She fled before the tiger could realize the prey had left the room.

Three

Danica wasn't quite sure what to expect from her dinner with Luke, but this establishment wasn't it. Surely white tablecloths and waiters wearing black tie were more his style? She glanced at her new phone and re-read the email. This was the address. She looked up at the dingy neon sign that appeared as if it hadn't been cleaned since first put into place decades ago. That was the name of the restaurant. Squaring her shoulders, she looked past the layers of graffiti decorating the outside walls and stepped inside.

The taqueria's interior was reminiscent of an ancient cafeteria, with laminate white tables and red plastic chairs lined up on the scuffed black-and-white-checkerboard linoleum floor. A long line of people stood in front of a high counter, orders barked in rapid

Spanish and English. The smell of freshly made tortillas and the sound of knives chopping tomatoes and peppers reminded her stomach how long it had been since she ate a protein bar at her desk.

At least she wouldn't be underdressed as she'd feared. Her cream polyester blouse and navy skirt would allow her to blend right into the disparate crowd. She stood off to the side of the front entrance to wait for Luke, her gaze wandering over the restaurant. The wide range of patrons, from teenagers to executives, made it a prime opportunity for people watching. She smiled as a young mother wrangled her toddler by offering him torn pieces of tortilla. But her attention was arrested by a tall, powerfully built man waiting in line to order, his well-worn jeans molded to the tight, muscular curves of his rear end.

Just then, the man turned and waved at her. She quickly glanced away, ashamed to be caught ogling.

"Danica," he called, "over here."

It took her a moment to realize the perfect male rear draped in vintage Levi's belonged to her boss.

She swallowed. Who knew he had been hiding that under his usual khakis? And she had to admit his front view was just as nice as the back. A dark blue shirt matched his eyes despite the tendency of the overhead fluorescent lights to turn every color to a greenish yellow. His hair was swept back and damp, a testament to a recent shower. As if to confirm her suspicions, when she got into line with him she caught of whiff of soap along with his unique scent.

"There you are," he said. "Do you know what you

want?" He pointed to the large menu board over their heads. "They're famous for their burritos. But if you want something else, go for it." He flashed his killer smile at her, and her stomach turned several flips.

"A burrito sounds fine," she said, after trying to read the board and failing because the words wouldn't stick in her brain. Not with Luke's nearness occupying all the other senses. "Whatever you suggest. But easy on the hot sauce. Nonexistent easy."

He raised a skeptical eyebrow. "Is eating here okay? We could go somewhere else if this isn't to your taste." His tone implied not enjoying Mexican food was incomprehensible, like still believing in the tooth fairy.

She shook her head. "I like to try new foods. I just have a New England palate, that's all."

"Anything else I should know? Vegetarian? Food sensitivities? Anaphylactic shock caused by peanuts?"

She laughed. He grinned back at her, his expression more relaxed than she had ever seen it. "Peanuts? Just what is in this burrito? No, no other restrictions," she said.

He nodded and began a conversation with the man behind the counter in rapid, fluid Spanish. Luke accepted two long-necked Mexican beers with one hand and used the other to guide her to a nearby table.

She sat down in a red plastic chair. It was just a business dinner with her boss. Something she and Johanna used to do on a regular basis. Only Johanna never made her pulse sing an aria just by touching her elbow.

She cleared her throat. "What's our number? I'll fetch the food."

"Don't have to," Luke said. He pushed one of the beers in front of her and then took a deep swallow from his. "Enrique will bring the food to us."

She looked around. No one else was receiving table service. All the other patrons went to the counter to bring back trays packed high with plastic baskets filled with foil-wrapped food and tortilla chips. "Another perk of being the CEO of Ruby Hawk?"

He frowned. "Because I'm CEO? No. But because of Ruby Hawk?" He used his beer bottle to indicate a boisterous group of teenage boys, joking with each other as they dug into their food. Each one wore a bright gold basketball jersey, with a small red bird emblazoned on the front. They reminded her of her brother. "You could say that. We sponsor the league, while Enrique lets this team eat here on game days. Enrique got the worse bargain."

She smiled. Feeding an active teenage boy was something her family knew well. Or at least they used to. "I bet. Was the league your previous commitment?"

"How did you know?"

She indicated his damp hair. "I doubt a business meeting would require shampoo after." A vision of him standing under a shower jet, water cascading off that flawless rear end hidden under his jeans, steam rising off the smooth biceps peeking out from the sleeves of his T-shirt, nearly caused her to choke on her beer. She put the bottle down and ducked under the table to rummage in her tote bag.

Once she was sure the color in her face had returned to normal, she resurfaced, a file folder in her hand.

"So," she said, attempting to sound brisk and professional, "as I said earlier, you were right. I hadn't looked
outside the box. These candidates—" she slid the folder
over to him "—should be more to your specifications."

He pushed the folder away. "Maybe. But I never discuss business while hungry. It leads to poor decision-
making. Speaking of, here comes our food." The man
who took their order placed a tray on their table, carrying on another conversation in Spanish with Luke
that ended with both men laughing and shaking hands.
When he left, Luke turned back to Danica. "Dig in."

Luke sat back in his chair. The stress that caused his
shoulders to be in a perpetual knot since his meeting
with Nestor was currently at bay, thanks to coaching
a hard-fought basketball game that helped focus his
mind outside his company. And, he had to admit: he
liked watching Danica's reactions.

She glanced around the taqueria, smiling at the other
patrons. He noticed it lingered the longest on the youth
basketball team, her expression somewhat wistful, before she turned her attention to her food. He was about
to ask her why when she let out a small groan.

"This burrito? Is amazing." She took another bite.
The look on her face was pure pleasure. He wondered
what else would cause that expression to appear and
found himself shifting in his seat.

"It's even better with salsa," he warned, taking his
own bite of the cheese-beans-and-rice-filled concoc-
tion.

"No way," she said with a sigh of contentment, and

took a long drink from her beer. His gaze fixated on her mouth, her plump lips wrapped around the neck of the bottle. When she swallowed, it caused an answering pull in his groin. Good thing she couldn't see under the table.

She caught his gaze with hers. Her eyes were more than just green, he noticed. Flecks of gold rimmed her pupils, while a band of forest green encircled her irises. What if he were to reach across the table, cover her luscious mouth with his, see if he could make those eyes darken to emerald...

She tore her gaze away, snapping the connection. The haze enveloping him dissipated. He sat back in his chair and stirred his salsa with a tortilla chip. *Analyze the situation. Don't let it control you*, he admonished himself.

He was having a physiological reaction to an attractive woman. It was understandable. His last relationship, if it could be called that, had ended three months ago and the quest to find new capital for Ruby Hawk had taken over his time and concentration since then. He liked sex and he missed having it.

But it wouldn't be with Danica. Yes, she had arresting eyes as well as tantalizing curves under her clothes that begged to be explored. And her brain was pretty damn appealing too. She was smart and perceptive, with a fast wit he enjoyed. He respected the way she stood up for her work in his office. And he was glad she accepted his invitation to dinner. They could have easily talked in the office the following morning. But he didn't want to wait to hear her insights, watch her gaze sharpen as she arrived at a new conclusion.

Still, she was his recruiter. For his wife, damn it. An affair with his consultant would not be a sensible prelude to a marriage. For all that he resented the situation Nestor had put him in, it did bring up a point Luke needed to think about sooner rather than later for maximum benefit. What good was creating a legacy if one didn't have offspring to carry it on? But unlike his parents and their multiple trips down the aisle, his marriage would be based on intellectual compatibility, similar upbringings and mutually agreed-upon goals. Should they come to an agreed-upon parting of the ways, it would be because common sense and rational prudence demanded it.

He popped the tortilla chip into his mouth. It made a satisfying crunch.

He still wanted to kiss Danica though.

She cleared her throat, a rosy glow high on her cheekbones, before placing the file folder in front of him once more. "So. Now that we're no longer hungry, can we discuss my work?"

"Fine." He opened the folder and ran his gaze down the list of fifteen names before closing it and handing it back to her. "No."

"What?" she sputtered. "I did what you asked. None of the women work in tech, and they meet your education and work-experience requirements. Yet you barely looked at it."

"I invited you here so you could have the correct input for your job. This list precedes our dinner. Therefore, it's inherently flawed," he pointed out with impeccable logic.

She took a deep breath and exhaled slowly. "Let's start over and pretend this is an actual executive search. Why is this position now open? What is the business rationale?" When he hesitated, she gave him a quick smile. "Confidential, remember? I signed an NDA."

It still smarted to know he'd miscalculated so poorly, but Danica's judgment-free gaze soothed some of the sting. He cleared his throat. "Nestor and Irene Stavros… The closest word is blackmail."

She blinked at him. Her pen didn't move. "Of all the things I expected to hear, that didn't make the top one thousand."

"Irene and I…" Used each other for sex when no one else was around? Were friends with only one benefit? It sounded crass even to think.

"Had a fling," Danica supplied. When he raised an eyebrow, the spots of color returned to her cheeks. "I did a thorough internet search on you. For work purposes only," she hastened to add.

"Had a fling," he agreed. It was close enough. "It started in college. It was off and on after that. However, when I started Ruby Hawk, I called it off for good."

"Any particular reason?"

"Does it matter?"

She gave him a stern look. It made her appear only more delectable. "I thought the purpose of this meeting was to give me the necessary input."

"Irene is very competitive. So am I. It's what drew

us together. We enjoyed one-upping one another. Taking turns on top. In and out of the…classroom."

Her tongue darted out to wet her lips. "I see," she murmured, bending her head over her pad.

"But when I discovered she wanted to extend our relationship—and competition—to Ruby Hawk, that was enough for me."

"Let me guess. If you avoid making decisions while hungry, then business and pleasure don't mix."

"Hunger is a chemical reaction in the brain. So is sex. As a rule, I avoid mind-altering stimulants in business." And he needed to keep that thought front and center. This was a business meeting. Not a prelude to wrapping her legs around him and evoking more of those moans.

Her gaze landed on his beer. He picked it up and took a swallow. "Alcohol is a social lubricant that puts many people at ease. I know my tolerance, so I'm able to observe the common niceties."

"Of course," she deadpanned. "Please, go on. You broke it off with Irene."

"And that was that. Until I sought growth opportunities for the company."

She frowned. "I'm not following."

"Ruby Hawk needs additional investment if we want to meet our benchmarks."

"I thought you were successful."

"We are. Very much so. But to fully reach our potential, we need to hire new staff, invest in new equipment. I've spent the last year researching investors or potential mergers. Then I received a call from Irene's father, Nestor." He frowned at his beer. He wished his tolerance weren't so high. It would be nice to have the edges filed off the jagged memory. "Ruby Hawk developed a revolutionary way to apply biofeedback technology to consumer entertainment. The Stavros Group is seeking to increase its global domination in the video-game industry. Incorporating our patents into their games would give players a whole new way to experience virtual worlds, while our R&D engineers would put them miles ahead of the competition. It's a slam dunk, businesswise."

Her eyes narrowed to a suspicious squint. "If it's a slam dunk and her father came to you, why is Irene blackmailing you?"

How to explain the twisted game his family and Irene's had played for decades? "I said blackmail was the closest word. It's not the most accurate."

Danica put her pen down. "I can't help if you aren't straight with me."

"This isn't just about me and Irene. It goes back at least a generation, maybe more. It's not a secret my mother is a Durham."

Her face was blank. "I don't know what that means."

"The Durhams were one of the first families to make their fortune in San Francisco during the gold rush. They helped rebuild the city after the 1906 earthquake. For a profit, of course. But by the time my mother was born, the Durham fortune was gone."

"Then why do the websites make a big deal about—" she waved a hand in the air "—y'know."

"My money?"

She nodded, shrugging her shoulders in an apology.

"My great-grandfather on my father's side. He founded a chain of department stores. The chain failed. He also owned the land under the stores, and that was valuable. Very valuable."

"Got it. Where does Irene come in?"

He briefly looked up at the ceiling. Nestor's trap still prickled with the sting of ten thousand red-hot pins. "My mother was engaged to Nestor Stavros. She broke it off with Nestor the night before the wedding and ran away with my father. See, Nestor hadn't made his money yet, but my father stood to inherit millions. However, he wasn't invited to join the right country clubs. She restored the Durham bank account and he got to play golf where he wanted."

Danica's mouth had been hanging slightly open. She closed it with a snap.

"Irene and I knew the family history." He laughed. There was no amusement in it. "It was probably what initially attracted us to each other. And Nestor didn't seem to care. I even interned for him when I was an undergrad at Stanford. When he approached me about acquiring Ruby Hawk, it seemed like the rational answer to both our businesses' needs."

"But it wasn't," Danica said softly.

His mouth twisted. "No. He wants to take my company away from me. Like my father took my mother away from him."

It hurt to say the words out loud. He'd worked so hard to distance himself from the toxicity that surrounded him growing up, the constant stream of new stepparents and stepsiblings appearing and disappearing. He threw himself into writing code, the static language reassuring even as he manipulated it to do new things. To have control of his legacy be threatened thanks to a marriage that barely survived his birth… He took a deep breath and returned his focus to his companion.

Danica pursed her lips into a kissable heart shape. "Wait. Did he say those exact words? Out loud? Because if the deal makes as much sense for both companies as you say it does, how can he justify that to his board of directors?" She launched into a respectable Australian accent. "Oi, I'm acquiring a company because I was jilted thirty years ago. Good on me?"

He took another swig of beer to wash down the memory of the meeting with Nestor, the anger burning hotter than any salsa could. "Funny you say that. Nestor said his board of directors insisted on a morals clause in the deal. If I don't meet the board's standards within sixty days, then either the Stavros Group can pull out of the deal or I will be removed from the company. My reputation for, as Nestor put it, 'loving and leaving' means I'm too unstable, too incapable of commitment for the Stavros Group to bring me onboard."

"Unsteady?" Her gaze widened in disbelief. "Luke Dalek?"

He toasted her with his beer for using his nickname. "When I protested, he brought in Irene. She backed him up, listing the times I supposedly used her and then walked away. She failed to mention our relationship, such as it was, had been mutual, including the breakups."

Danica squinted at him. "That sounds like she was upset you ended it. Are you sure this is about your mother's relationship with Nestor? Or is it really about you and Irene?"

His gut twisted. He dismissed it. He knew what he knew. "I'm positive this is retaliation for the past. But I'm not giving up Ruby Hawk. I'm running it, and that's nonnegotiable."

Visions of unpaid bills, the result of ordering equipment before the deal closed, danced before his eyes. He'd never be able to find another investor or potential buyer in time to make payroll. Hundreds of people depended on him for their livelihoods. He had a responsibility to them. He couldn't cause the deal to fail.

But if he didn't meet the Stavros Group's conditions, then he would be removed from the company he founded. The company into which he poured sweat and toil and sleepless nights. The legacy he hoped to leave, taken away. His best chance of proving he was more than his family's name and his inherited wealth.

He slammed down the empty bottle, causing Danica to jump. At least he didn't break the bottle. He wanted to. He wanted to smash it, then grind the pieces into dust.

She reached out a hand and briefly brushed the back of his. "Everyone knows Ruby Hawk is a success because of you."

He took a deep breath, his emotions settling back into their usual, well-ordered positions. "My lawyers and I did a thorough reading of the clause," he said. "In short, if I do not quote 'curtail my libidinous life-style' end quote, by the end of sixty days, then either the Stavros Group can pull out of the deal or the acquisition will go through but I will be removed. The only surefire way to fulfill the terms of the clause is to be married. A real marriage, not a pretend fiancée for a few months."

Danica blinked. "Wow. That's extreme."

"That's Nestor. Therefore, if I have to be married, I need a wife who is equipped to deal with the pressures that come with my world. That's where you come in."

Danica leaned back in her chair, her gaze fixed on the ceiling. He couldn't help but notice how her posture caused her silky blouse to drape tightly over her breasts. The fabric strained against the high, round globes, just the right size to fill his palms—no. Not his. He liked her, yes. But she was not the solution the situation required, but the means to the solution. His company and its future came ahead of any momentary personal pleasure.

"So," she said slowly, as if thinking through a problem, "if you're willing to go to the trouble of hiring me to find you a stranger to marry so the acquisition will go through, why not marry Irene?"

The beer in his stomach roiled. "I asked. She laughed in my face. This is about taking my company away, period." He crumbled his napkin and threw it into the now-empty plastic basket. "You now have the background. Let's discuss how you will find the right candidates. There are fifty-two days remaining."

"I have to admit, when you said I needed additional information, I thought you meant food preferences, favorite vacation spots, et cetera." She blew a loose curl off her forehead.

"Our discussion should make your job easier, not harder."

She laughed, a sharp burst of air. "You have that flipped." She took her wallet out of her purse and offered him a twenty-dollar bill. "I hope this covers my dinner?"

He pushed the money back at her. "That's too much and besides, the company paid. Why is it harder?"

She left the cash on the table. "So far, you've told me about you, your family and the Stavroses. What about the wife I'm supposed to find? Where does she fit into this?"

It was a good question. He'd been so focused on the terms of the acquisition, he hadn't thought beyond standing in front of a justice of the peace. He said the first thing that came to mind. "She'll be well compensated."

Her gaze widened with what he could only call horror. "Money doesn't make a marriage," she stated, her syllables crisp and precise.

He shrugged. "I beg to differ."

She leaned over the table, blond curls tumbling over her left shoulder, her words intense and fast. "When the war broke out in Croatia, my mother and father gave up everything to be together. Their families, their country, their religious communities. They came to the United

States with barely a dime. But they had love, and that made us richer than most people I knew growing up."

Luke blinked, once. He had no idea her parents had been war refugees. "That's admirable. It takes strength to start a new life."

Her features relaxed into a smile, a ray of sun peeking from behind a dark cloud. "Thank you. And love is what gave them that strength—"

"It's a good story. For them. But in my experience, marriage is best viewed a merger between two parties who desire a joint investment." He shrugged. "Usually in children. But the parties also need to protect their individual assets. The right candidate will know that." He gave the folder a decisive tap.

Danica rubbed her temples. She rarely got headaches, but it felt like a woodpecker and a jackhammer had had a baby in her skull, and the baby was throwing a tantrum. Luke couldn't really believe the words coming out of his mouth.

Could he?

"I thought…" She paused. In the aftermath of their conversation, her assumptions seemed so naïve. "I thought you wanted to fall in love with someone. That's why you hired me."

"It's business. That's why I hired an executive recruiter."

"But…love. Don't you want that?"

He looked as if he pitied her. "Humans confuse endorphins released during sex for love, and then they use the confusion to manipulate themselves and others.

But it's just a chemical reaction caused by hormones and preprogrammed neurological responses." He held up a hand to stop her before she could speak. "I know. Your family. But trust me. I've seen my scenario play out far more times than I've seen yours."

How did someone with everything going for him— gorgeous looks, genius brain, socially prominent family, Midas's wealth—have such a cynical outlook? It made her soul physically ache. She took her phone out of her tote and opened up the rideshare app.

"I'll have another list of candidates for you in the morning." She swept her notebook into the bag and pulled the bag's strap over her shoulder as she stood up. "Thank you for dinner. I'll see you tomorrow?"

He stood up when she did. "I'd like to discuss this tonight. The clock is running."

The drumming in her skull would make a death-metal band proud. "Your criteria haven't changed, so I'll fine-tune the parameters. The difference will come in how I conduct interviews, to see if I can suss out if their attitude toward marriage matches yours." She tried to smile but was only partially successful. "I'll email you the list of candidates tonight, so you'll have it in the morning. Thanks again for the burrito."

She turned on her heel and exited the restaurant, heading for the nearest street corner. The car she had ordered via the phone app should arrive soon to take her to the train station. And not a minute too early.

How could he not want love? It was a basic human need, as necessary as sunshine and clean water. She knew people married for all sorts of reasons, love being only one of them, but it seemed so...*cold-blooded* the way he'd spelled it out.

"Danica, wait." Footsteps pounded on the sidewalk behind her.

She tamped down on the traitorous anticipation swirling in her stomach and turned to face him. "Did I leave something at the restaurant?"

He stepped under the streetlight. The mist-filled night air caused it to create a halo around his head. The very picture of an angelic devil.

"I know what you're thinking." He ran a hand through his hair, causing it to stick straight-up in patches. It made him look only more approachable and thus more attractive. "You think I'm doing this because of some long-standing feud. And maybe you're right. But I'm also doing this for my team. I hand recruited them. They took stock options instead of salary when we started. Now they can cash in on their leap of faith. I'm not being as ruthless as you think I am."

He moved closer, tripping her pulse into overdrive. "That's not what I'm thinking," she said.

He gave her a one-sided smile. "You're easier to read than you know."

Fine. She *had* been thinking that. She glanced over his shoulder and saw the youth basketball team exit the taqueria. The teenagers were laughing and horsing around as they said their goodbyes. It was a scene she had seen many times before, with her brother at the center of the action. Now her family didn't know if Matt would be able to walk unassisted ever again.

Her parents showed her love was real, but they also

taught her family came first. If she successfully completed the search, the money Luke offered would give them much needed relief from financial worry. In a way, she was in just as much of a bind as he was.

Besides, judging by the way he talked about his team, he was capable of caring—if only as the boss.

"I know what it's like to have your dream job disappear. For your team, I'll do my best. But if I can be honest? Any marriage entered into under the conditions you describe is doomed to failure."

"I never fail." A self-satisfied smirk played at the corners of his devastatingly attractive mouth.

"There's always a first time."

He leaned down until his warm breath caressed her cheek. "We'll see."

An answering heat welled deep inside her, an insistent compulsion she needed to stop before she did something stupid, like use her hands to determine if his butt felt as muscular as it looked in his jeans. Thankfully, a car matching the description on her app pulled up to the curb. "That's my ride."

She turned to say good-night at the same minute he reached to open the car door for her. They collided, her breasts colliding with the hard planes of his chest. She instinctively grabbed on to his biceps to hold herself steady, while his arms encircled her.

Their gazes met, held. She couldn't get enough air in her lungs. "Sorry," he began.

She shook her head, once. The fog swirled around them, shutting the world out until it consisted of just him, her and the awareness between them that could no longer be ignored. His gaze turned heavy, matching the heaviness between her legs, asking a question she answered by reaching up to bring his mouth down to hers.

He responded immediately, his lips firm, hot, insistent. Supernovas pinwheeled behind her closed eyelids as his hands settled at her waist and drew her closer.

She had wanted to kiss Luke Dallas since she saw him outside Johanna's office. She doubted she could break away even if the sensible part of her brain managed to gain control. It had been so long since she had last been kissed.

His tongue licked into her mouth, and she returned the favor. Her pulse thumped hard as his firm arms tightened around her. She heard a low moan and realized it came from her. Her skin needed to be next to his, the insistent desire building deep inside demanding to be fed.

A car horn, loud and insistent, broke through the pleasurable haze surrounding her. She jumped away from him, raising a wondering hand to her swollen lips.

He stared back at her, hands thrust into his jeans pockets, his gaze dark and wild.

The horn honked again. Danica wrenched her gaze away from Luke to glance at the vehicle. "I need to go."

Luke nodded. "Right. So." He cleared his throat. "I'll see you in the office. Safe travels home."

She nodded back. "See you in the office." Somehow, she managed to slide into the back seat and sped off. Her last sight of Luke was him standing on the sidewalk, hands in his pockets, staring after her car.

Her mouth still bore the imprint of his, her core aching from unresolved need. Her thoughts twisted and churned, mimicking the roiling in her stomach. She'd kissed Luke! And he'd kissed her back. It exceeded any fantasy she'd ever had. For a second she basked in the recollection, reliving the pressure, the heat, the demand for more.

Then a tsunami of horror washed away the joyous memory. What had they done? He'd hired her. She'd agreed to find him a wife. She needed the contract and the money it promised for her family. Did she just risk her job and thus her brother's access to treatment?

How would she be able to face Luke in the morning?

Her lips would not stop burning.

Four

Danica walked the last few steps toward the main entrance of Ruby Hawk, her stomach doing a decent impersonation of a tumble dryer set on high. What would she say to Luke after their kiss last night? More important, what would he say to her?

It was unprofessional to kiss a client in the best of circumstances. And this client was Luke Dallas, bad-boy billionaire of Silicon Valley, known for his countless flings with models, actresses and socialites. It wasn't only unseemly; it was downright embarrassing.

But he kissed you back. His mouth opened first, his tongue invited hers to tangle and slide against his. She couldn't recall arriving home or getting into bed, but she remembered the perfect firmness of his mouth— not too hard, not too soft—and how his hand on the small of her back had burned through the silk of her blouse. She stumbled on a crack in the pavement and regained her balance at the last second.

It wasn't as if she hadn't been kissed before, she scolded herself. She was very familiar with the mechanics. No need to be so dramatic.

She managed to make it to her office without twisting an ankle and turned on her computer. A message from Luke sat at the top of her email inbox. Her hand lingered over the mouse for a second before she took a deep breath and clicked to open it.

It was short and to the point.

I trust you now have the necessary information to find viable candidates. I'm on a flight to Tokyo but I expect a new list by the time I land.

Any lingering warmth was doused. She clicked on Reply.

Thank you for the dinner. Your input has been taken under advisement as requested.

She attached the list she pulled together when last night's sleep eluded her and hit Send. Really, it was the best of all possible outcomes. She was still employed and could still secure the bonus money he promised her. But when lunchtime rolled around, she realized she couldn't remember a single email she'd read other than Luke's.

The next two weeks were spent chasing leads, the

kiss eventually fading from her lips but playing on a continuous loop whenever she shut her eyes. Luke was mostly out of town. He jetted around the world, seeking a backup for the acquisition in case Nestor Stavros reneged as threatened. However, her speech about communication seemed to have sunk in, because he was quick to respond to a text or an email despite any time difference. Before long, the ding of a new text or email arriving became her favorite sound.

She began the Monday of the third week with a satisfied sigh. Two of her candidates finally met Luke's standards. He met the first one upon his return to California and immediately asked to see her again. While she was waiting to hear his feedback from the latest encounter, she went ahead and finalized the arrangements for him to meet the second candidate. All she needed was a third prospective wife, and then she would be out the door with an impressive check in hand and her professional integrity intact.

There was only one glaring problem with completing her assignment. Success meant she'd no longer communicate with Luke. She may have buried the kiss, never to be spoken of again although it starred in her most erotic dreams, but she didn't know if she could bury how much she looked forward to their daily exchanges.

She opened a text message window and typed a message to Luke.

All confirmed for tonight. Felicity Sommers will meet you at seven at the Peninsula Society fund-raiser in

Atherton. I told her this is a callback for the community-giving job, and you want to meet her there so the two of you can discuss best practices.

Danica had realized early on she needed a cover story for her search. She couldn't tell the candidates up front they were being vetted as a possible wife for Luke Dallas—not if she wanted to keep the search out of the press. Therefore she told the women she was looking for a director to run Ruby Hawk's community outreach and charitable giving. The job *was* open, so it wasn't completely a lie.

The rest was up to Luke. Thinking of him walking down the aisle with his recruited-to-order wife caused her heart to do flips, and not the pleasant kind. The kind that ended with every surface bruised and battered.

Her computer dinged.

Consider this confirmation of my meeting with Felicity. Remove Jayne Chung from consideration.

Danica frowned at her screen. Jayne was the first candidate Luke had agreed to meet. On paper, she was perfect: Harvard educated, did a stint in the Peace Corps before receiving her master's degree in urban planning and development, and currently worked for a nonprofit providing grants to create city gardens where none existed. Oh, and she'd paid for her education by modeling haute couture in New York and Paris during school breaks.

I thought the first meeting went well. What's wrong?
She didn't start the second meeting by swooning at
your feet?

Ha.

I think kids these days say LOL.

    He ignored her attempt at levity.

She's not right for the position.

    If Jayne wasn't right…

More input, please.

    A wave of heat settled deep in her belly at the mem-
ory of just how visceral his input could be. *Help me
help you.*
    No answer. She sat back in her chair. Usually he
texted her back, even if it was just a curt Later.
    She sighed and shut down the text window. There
was a simple reason why he didn't respond: he ran a
billion-dollar tech company and she was a consultant
hired for one task.
    Speaking of, if his reaction to Jayne were any in-
dication, she would need the third candidate sooner
rather than later. Danica had liked Felicity, Luke's current date, well enough when they met during the initial
vetting period. But something had been a little…off.

Felicity had set off a tiny warning light in the back of Danica's mind.

She shook her head. All that mattered was Luke's reaction to Felicity. Danica needed to stay focused, finish the assignment and concentrate on helping her brother. The kiss would eventually fade. Eventually. She absorbed herself in answering emails and chasing down promising leads online.

The phone rang, dragging her gaze away from her screen. She looked at the time. 6:45 p.m. Well, that settled it. No more texting with Luke tonight. He should be handing his car keys to the valet at the fund-raiser right about now. A vision of Luke in a tuxedo, the fine black wool jacket tailored to emphasize his broad shoulders, caused her to almost drop the phone before she could answer it. "Hello?"

"Danica! Thank goodness you picked up."

"Aisha?" Her favorite investigator sounded panicked. And nothing panicked Aisha McKee. "What's wrong?"

"Felicity Sommers. We have a problem."

That tiny warning light put out a full red alert. "What kind of a problem?"

Aisha sighed. "I saw something today on her social media that made me ask around. Turns out she's engaged. Has been for a month. But they haven't told her parents, so they're keeping it quiet."

"What?" Danica's stomach dropped somewhere near her knees. "That's bad."

"It gets worse." Aisha audibly inhaled. "Her fiancé? Cinco Jackson."

"Cinco Jackson—wait. I know that name." Danica opened a browser window to the *Silicon Valley Weekly* website, clicked on the top story and then shut her eyes, tight. "He's the journalist responsible for the recent Ruby Hawk stories."

"Yeah." Aisha sighed again. "I'm sorry it took me until now to discover the relationship. Turns out her parents are dead set against it because one of his previous stories was an exposé that took down a friend of her father's, so they keep it very low-key. One of Felicity's former sorority sisters filled me in."

Danica replayed the conversations she had with Felicity. No, she didn't mention marriage. She and Luke agreed he would broach the until-death-do-us-part subject when he felt it was right.

She had to warn him. If he let something slip to Felicity and it got back to Jackson…

"I have to go." Danica shut down her laptop. "Thanks for the warning. Talk to you soon."

"Sorry again," Aisha started to say, but Danica hit End before she'd finished and dialed Luke's number. No answer. Great. She ordered a car while keeping Luke's number on redial. If he didn't pick up his phone, she had only one option: get to him in person as quickly as possible.

The Aylward-Hopkins mansion hummed with laughter and conversation as the cream of the Bay Area elite enjoyed the Peninsula Society's annual Monte Carlo Night. Croupiers spun roulette wheels, the wheel clack-clacking until the ball dropped with a soft metallic thud, while dice rattled against green felt at the craps tables. Although the games of chance were played with faux money, the charity expected its silent auction to bring in over five hundred thousand dollars to help fund its grants for the next year.

Luke stood in the expansive entry of the mansion, a space big enough that it easily accommodated one of the bars set up for thirsty guests. From his position, he could keep an eye on the front door and new arrivals but also survey the gaming tables occupying the long sweep of travertine floors just beyond the entry. French windows lined the opposite wall, their doors open to the mild night air and the sprawling gardens beyond.

Normally, he'd rather waste hours trying to code on an ancient Apple II Plus computer than put on a monkey suit and pretend to be interested in a retired captain of industry's golf game. He sat on the charity's board, which should be enough demonstration of his support. But he knew from observing his parents that strategic networking at social events was almost as crucial to success in business as a good product. His presence here tonight was a simple equation of trade-offs and benefits.

A member of the catering staff in a low-cut black dress offered him a glass of champagne. He took it off the silver tray and she smiled at him, giving him a slow wink as she brushed by a bit too close for social propriety.

At any other time, Luke might have been interested. But he was here to meet…what was her name? Right. Felicity.

Too bad it wasn't Danica.

He did a quick calculation of the probabilities, as he did every time her green eyes crossed his mind. Which meant he ran this particular set of calculations on an hourly, if not even more frequent, basis. But his initial assessment always came out on top. Danica didn't have the right variables he required.

Yes, she was smart. And he liked her assertiveness. Plus, she made him laugh. Her humor shone through in her texts and emails.

Nonetheless, statistical outcomes for maximum marriage success as measured by length of time married as plotted against divorce rates demonstrated he should stick to his original requirements for education, social status and career achievement.

But…

That kiss. She'd fit against him just the way he liked, her curves connecting with his body in all the right spots. Pure responsiveness, hot and genuine, the heat flaring spontaneously. And that moan, low and breathy, when she'd pressed against him… He'd had to walk multiple blocks in the chilly night air before he was comfortable enough to drive home.

If he wasn't careful, the memory would require leaving the party for a similar stroll. He took out his phone to distract himself just as a pretty redhead, more auburn than strawberry blonde, came through the front door. She looked around and when her gaze met his, she gave him a small wave. He nodded at her over his champagne and put the phone, still off, back in his pocket.

He had to give Danica credit. The first candidate had more than met his criteria, and so far, Felicity also seemed like a good match. She wore a navy blue gown appropriate for the occasion, elegantly simple. Her smile was bright and easily given, her handshake firm as they greeted each other. She had no trouble meeting his gaze, her eyes a greenish brown.

Danica's eyes were green. A warm green with flecks of gold. When her temper rose, they transformed to dark emerald. He liked she hadn't hid her reactions during their dinner. She'd expressed them, fully. And when they'd kissed—

With a start, he realized Felicity was speaking. He tuned in just in time to hear her say, "Thank you so much for inviting me to the fund-raiser. I've heard a lot about Monte Carlo Night."

He cleared his throat. "Thank you for accepting." He caught the gaze of the waitress who had given him his champagne and motioned her over. "Something to drink?"

Felicity hesitated. "I have an early morning meeting. I shouldn't—but sure. Thanks." She accepted the glass with a smile from the less-friendly-than-before waitress. "I've never had champagne at a job interview before." She laughed. "But then I've never had an interview at a black-tie event."

"It's unorthodox. But this is an unusual employment offer." There was something in the way Felicity's gaze flashed when he said *unusual* that made him reconsider saying anything further. "Tell me about your job at Friedmann Adams. What's your favorite thing about it?"

He ignored the urge to look at his watch to see how much longer he needed to stay at the party and still be considered socially polite. Leaving early wouldn't be productive, nor help him accomplish his goals for the evening. If Felicity didn't work out, Danica had to provide only one more preapproved candidate before her contract terminated.

Danica...

He smiled, remembering their conversation after that dinner and how she'd tried to pretend he didn't know what she was thinking. It had been written all over her expressive face. Not that he blamed her for believing in fairy tales like love and living happily ever after. They were pervasive in the prevailing culture. But they were emotional manipulations. Insubstantial.

Sex, on the other hand, was an actual physical phenomenon. It could be scientifically studied. What would it be like if he studied it with Da—

"And that's the difference between a pessimist, an optimist and a financial advisor!" Felicity laughed. "That pretty much sums up what I do."

He'd missed most of it. What was wrong with his focus? "Fascinating."

Felicity pushed a strand of hair behind her right ear and glanced around the temporary casino. The gaming tables were filling up, and the polished travertine floor meant the sound level rose accordingly. "Not really. I could tell by the way you weren't on the edge of your seat."

Caught. "It's noisy in here," he said. "Let's find a quieter spot."

"That would be great. I'd like that." She gave him a generous smile.

Her lips were full and softly curved. But he had no desire to kiss them. Didn't care to learn how she tasted. No interest in discovering how her mouth would feel against his or if her response would be soft and quivering or hard and driving.

There was only one person he wanted to kiss, and that was—

His peripheral vision caught someone frantically waving two arms high in the air. *Danica?*

For a second, he wondered if his undisciplined subconscious had conjured a vision of her. But then a grin lit her face as their gazes met, and he knew it really was her.

No memory could be that vibrant. The details that had become fuzzy over the past few weeks now appeared in solid form. Her hair, so many different colors of gold, the curls tumbling from her ponytail, twisting and turning in the light. The way she walked, her rounded hips slightly swaying as she cut through the crowd with graceful deliberation.

Her eyes matched his memory exactly. They shone with some unexpressed emotion. Was she happy to see him? Or—no. Something was wrong. He narrowed his gaze questioningly as she arrived at his side. She shook her head slightly in response and thrust her left hand toward Felicity.

"Hi!" she said, her voice as bright as the artificial smile on her face. "Nice to meet you again."

Felicity shook the proffered hand, but a crease dented her brow. "Likewise. I didn't know you were going to be here."

"Of course! I wouldn't miss this event for the world."

Felicity ran her gaze up and down Danica's outfit. Her nose wrinkled as if she saw something not to her liking, which was ridiculous. Danica looked beautiful. She had forgone her usual skirt-and-blouse combo for a plain black dress with buttons down the front, like an oversize men's shirt, belted at the waist. He appreciated the way it emphasized her curves. "I see," Felicity said slowly.

"Oh," Danica said with a strained laugh, brushing her palms against the skirt of her dress, "I ran here straight from work. Hope I haven't already missed too much." She turned to Luke. "What have you two been talking about?" Her eyes were opened wide, as if she were trying to send him a message.

"Felicity told a joke about the difference between optimists, pessimists and financial advisors," he said. At least he assumed it had been a joke.

"I'd love to hear it someday." Danica kept her gaze focused on Luke. He didn't mind. "Did you talk about the open position?"

"No," Felicity said. Luke jerked his head in her direction. He'd almost forgotten she was still standing there. "We did not. I have some questions I'd like to ask."

"I'm sure you do." Danica finally took her gaze

away from Luke. The absence hit him like bedcovers yanked off on a cold winter's morning. "That's why I'm here. To help answer them. But—" She stopped, her gaze focused on a point over Felicity's shoulder. "Hey, isn't that Cinco Jackson over by the bar? You know, the business reporter for the *Silicon Valley Weekly*? I love his work." Danica waved at the reporter, who remained focused on his drink.

What the hell was she doing, trying to attract the attention of a journalist? Was that why she was here? His gut said no, but he suddenly realized he and Danica hadn't really spoken since the kiss. And they needed to. It was way out of bounds for him to kiss a contractor. He couldn't and wouldn't blame her if she went to the press despite the NDA. "Danica, can we talk first—"

She trod on his toe. Good thing she wore flat black shoes that looked like ballet slippers. "Hmm, he's not looking our way. I'd love to meet him. I don't suppose you know him, Felicity?"

Two spots of red appeared on Felicity's cheeks. "As a matter of fact, I do."

"You're so lucky!" Danica gushed. "I heard from a friend of a friend—on the down low, mind you—that he's engaged. I'm so jealous."

Jealous? What the… He opened his mouth, only for Danica's heel to connect with his foot again. "Felicity, are you okay?" Danica asked. "Did your champagne go down the wrong way?"

Felicity was indeed sputtering. "Engaged?" she managed to get out. "Where did you hear that? No one knows—" She clamped her lips shut.

Danica clasped a hand to her chest, her eyes wide with amazement. "It is true?" she gasped. "But how do you... Oh! Don't tell me! You must be the fiancée!"

Luke managed to move his shoe before Danica could step on it once more. "I gather best wishes are in order," he said, shooting a warning glance at Danica. She needed to cut back on the enthusiasm.

Not that Felicity seemed to notice Danica was over-doing it. The redhead resembled a fish realizing too late the baited hook had been swallowed. "I—I didn't confirm that."

Danica put a conciliatory hand on Felicity's arm. "Don't worry. We won't say anything."

"But I didn't—"

"You don't need to," Danica said. "You haven't stopped looking at Cinco Jackson since I mentioned him."

"I—" Felicity tore her gaze away from the reporter and shrugged. "Fine. It's true. And this is the strangest job interview I have ever been on."

"It is unusual," Danica agreed, her smile still five hundred watts bright.

"It's the Ruby Hawk way," Luke interjected. "If you're not comfortable in out-of-the-box situations, you won't be comfortable working with me."

"Out of the box certainly describes Luke's methods." Danica gave an emphatic nod.

"This was a test?" Felicity asked.

"Luke gets ambushed all the time by people wanting to pry confidential information out of him. We needed to see how you would react in a similar situation," Danica said smoothly. "Do you still have questions for us?"

Felicity's gaze ping-ponged between Luke and Danica. "I have a million, but not about the job. I think we all know I just took myself out of the running." She laughed, her shoulders falling. "It's actually a relief. I guess I can tell you now. Cinco just accepted an on-air job with a New York City station. We move in a few months."

Danica's smile disappeared. "Then why did you agree to the interview?"

"I was flattered. It's not every day you get a call out of the blue to discuss running a foundation. If the offer had been too good to refuse—" she shrugged "—who knows? I might have tried to work out a bicoastal arrangement."

Luke swirled the champagne in his glass. "Jackson didn't ask you to accept the interview in the hopes of getting inside information about Ruby Hawk?"

Felicity bit her lower lip.

Terrific. Thankfully, Danica saved the evening before he could dig himself into a pit too deep to get out of. He reached for her hand and gave her slender fingers a squeeze of appreciation.

Danica jumped, but kept her gaze on Felicity. "There's still a lot of Monte Carlo Night left. Why don't you find your fiancé and have fun?"

Felicity's gaze shifted between Luke and Danica a few more times. "I will. Oh, and, Luke, I know Cinco would love to talk to you—"

"We'll keep that in mind," Danica interjected. "Best

wishes for continued success with your career." She beamed at the other woman.

Felicity's mouth twisted. "Right. Well, thank you for the opportunity."

She moved to shake Luke's hand, but Danica maneuvered her way between him and Felicity. She intercepted Felicity's proffered hand with a shake of her own. "It was great meeting you. Have a terrific night!"

As soon as Felicity joined her fiancé, Danica's face fell. She turned to face Luke, her teeth worrying her lower lip. "I am so sorry. I had no idea she was engaged until my investigator called a little while ago. I hope this didn't ruin your evening."

He opened his mouth to reassure her.

Then he reconsidered. Danica was here, in person, not just a voice on the phone or a string of characters in a text message. And suddenly he was looking forward to an evening of socializing. With her.

He straightened his expression and looked down on her from his full height. "I'm out a date. At a black-tie event."

Danica kept her chin raised, but her gaze fell to the ground. "Yes, I know. I will find someone to replace Felicity. I still owe you two candidates."

"Doesn't help my situation right now."

"If I could change the situation, I would—" she began, her eyes wide with apology.

"Good. You're my date."

Five

Danica stared at him. "You want me to be your date? Here? Now?"

She swept her left hand to indicate the crowd dressed in expensive finery, the museum-quality artwork on the walls and the bottles of vintage French champagne being emptied and replaced by more. Then she swept her right hand over her plain shirtdress, a bargain from an outlet store two years ago. "Me?"

He shrugged. The movement emphasized how well his tuxedo jacket outlined his broad shoulders. "I RSVP'd for two. Beggars can't be choosers."

She narrowed her gaze and was about to tell him just how much of beggar he needed to be for her to stay when she caught the slight uptick of his mouth. "Very funny," she said.

"I think the kids say LOL."

She laughed and his grin appeared, his teeth flashing white against his bronzed skin. "You really want me to stay?"

He nodded, slowly and deliberately. "I do."

She'd heard stories from her previous boss about the Peninsula Society's Monte Carlo Night. The morning after previous years' events, Johanna would arrive hours late to work and then spend the day rhapsodizing about the gourmet food, the designer dresses and, above all, the one-of-a-kind silent-auction prizes that had millionaires trying to outbid each other, using chips won at the gaming tables augmented by very real money.

And now Danica was here. She glanced around at the glittering crowd and caught the gaze of a nearby server, who sniffed and rolled her eyes at Danica before she turned away to offer another guest a glass of champagne. This was Luke's world, she reminded herself. His and that of the wife he wanted her to find. Even the catering staff knew she didn't belong.

Her parents came to America thanks to a small grassroots organization dedicated to helping war refugees. But after her parents arrived and the novelty of welcoming refugees wore off, the organizers' interest waned. Her mother and father were left practically stranded, the promises of professional jobs as empty as the new bank accounts set up for them.

Her parents survived. They found work—not the positions promised, but they made enough money to rent an apartment and buy a fifteen-year-old car. Danica was born a year later. But her parents made sure she knew the story. *Only family can be trusted to look out for each other*, they warned her and her brother over and over.

Like she was doing now. Looking out for her brother, by finishing this assignment. Parties like this were an everyday occurrence for Luke, but they were the unobtainable fantasies of film and television to her. It would be better, when she said goodbye to him in a few weeks, if she stuck to her world and did not even visit his. One dinner and one kiss had consumed nearly every waking hour—and definitely every sleeping hour. A whole evening in his company? She'd never be able to return to reality.

"Thank you so much for the offer. But I should get back to the office. The clock is ticking on my assignment."

His smile dimmed. "If you insist. However…" His sideways glance caused her pulse to flutter.

"Yes?" she asked, using her tongue to wet her suddenly dry lips. Did he think about their kiss as often as she did?

"What cover story do you give your candidates?" he asked, his gaze fixed on her mouth. "And what is this event?"

"The community-giving job…and this is a society fund-raiser," she said slowly.

He nodded. "My wife will be involved with the Bay Area nonprofit community and its donors." He indicated the gaming tables. "And the biggest ones are here tonight. As your client, I advise it's in your best interests to stay so your cover story for the search will be as authentic as possible. This is business." His expression was impressively impassive.

"Business," she echoed. Of course. What else did she expect? She would show up and her presence would cause Prince Charming to admit he was attracted to her and throw away his careful calculations for the perfect wife? Fairy tales weren't real. If they were, her shirtdress would have transformed into a glittering ball gown a half hour ago.

"What else is there besides business?" The glint in his blue gaze dared her to answer.

If he wasn't going to mention their kiss, she certainly wasn't. "You're right," she said, her tone brisk. "My job is to find you a wife who will be comfortable at events like this."

"Precisely." He finished off his champagne. "Therefore, you need to stay in order to complete your assignment more effectively."

"If that's what the client prefers."

Luke's expression relaxed. It was the first time she'd seen him let down all of his guard. It made him impossibly appealing. Especially the warm, appreciative glow deep in his blue gaze, which lit an answering heat in her belly. "He does."

He placed his empty flute on a passing waiter's tray and took two new ones, offering one to her. She accepted it with a nod of thanks. The champagne tasted of bright, sharp honey. "So. What's first on the agenda?" she asked.

"Let's check out the gaming tables. For research purposes, of course." He offered her his elbow.

She'd never been a huge fan of the James Bond film franchise for various reasons, not the least of which was their tendency to make Eastern Europeans the bad guys. But now she understood why Bond had his contingents of female fans. Luke was already an attractive man. Put him in a tux and he was stunning. The fine wool of his jacket was soft to the touch above the firm muscle of his bicep. She kept her grip loose, not wishing to tempt her fingers into exploring what would never be hers. "Of course," she replied. "Let's go."

He escorted her to where the party organizers had arranged the gaming tables. They were organized in long rows, filling a large open space that overlooked the gardens below. Other guests had the same idea, and the seats were quickly filling up. "Pick your game," he said with a sweep of his hand.

She scanned the sea of green-felt-covered surfaces. While she didn't consider herself a gambler by any stretch of the definition, if she had to stay, she might as well enjoy herself. "Roulette," she said with a nod.

Luke had a slight frown on his face. "What's wrong?" she asked. "Not a fan of things that spin?"

He shrugged and began to guide her with an arm held low on her back toward the nearest wheel. Her shirt dress was a sturdy cotton weave, but the warmth of his touch burned as if he were touching her bare skin. "There's an approximate forty-seven percent chance of winning a bet placed on black or red, but low risk equals low reward. Playing a single number pays out the best, but the odds of winning are one in thirty-eight. Assuming the table isn't biased, of course," he said.

She stopped short, causing another couple to almost bump into them. The man started to give Danica a dirty look, but it turned into a nod of respect when he saw her companion. "How on earth do you know that?" she asked.

"There are thirty-eight numbers on an American roulette wheel. Thirty-seven if it's European. It doesn't take an MBA to calculate the odds."

She smirked at him. "Your math skills are not in question. How do you know this much about roulette? Do you play often?"

"I prefer playing with money when circumstances can be better controlled."

"That doesn't explain why you can rattle off the statistics."

His mouth twisted to the left. "I was given my first computer when I was ten. When I wanted to replace it with a newer one, my father decided to teach me one of his sporadic object lessons and told me I had to buy it myself. But he never told me how he expected me to come up with the money. So, I created an account for a gambling site using my stepmother's credit card." He smiled, but his gaze remained distant. "There were less restrictions on the internet then."

Her eyes felt dry. She was staring at him so hard she forgot to blink. "You started gambling. At ten."

"Eleven. Only to earn enough to buy a new computer." He thought for a moment. "And maybe some peripheral equipment. I stopped when I reached the amount I needed. But to answer your question, I prefer games that require strategy, such as blackjack or poker."

"What did your stepmother say when she discovered you used her card?" Her parents would have grounded her for at least a month if she had used a credit card without permission. Not that she could imagine doing such a thing in the first place. Her family always had food on the table, but money wasn't plentiful. She didn't get her first computer until a hand-me-down came her way during high school.

Luke paused. "She didn't say anything," he finally said. "I know I went to live with my mother, because I had the computer shipped to her house. It must have coincided with my father divorcing that stepmother."

"'That' stepmother? How many have you had?"

"Three. Stepmothers, that is. Four stepfathers. So far." Luke's gaze continued to search the busy crowd. "There," he said. "Empty seats at the third table from the left, toward the back." He resumed guiding her through the throng.

Danica let him take the lead, her mind still processing the glimpse he let slip. She couldn't imagine her parents with anyone else, much less multiple anyone elses. Yet Luke had—she did the addition in her head—nine parents, including his biological ones? No wonder he held such cynical views about marriage.

They took their places at the roulette wheel beside a woman who wore more diamonds than Danica had ever seen outside of a jewelry store. The woman raised her eyebrows when Danica squeezed next to her, but gave Luke a welcoming smile. He handed the croupier a slip of paper and received two large stacks of multi-colored casino chips in return.

"Here," he said, passing half of them to Danica. "When it comes to betting, I recommend the D'Alembert system. Start small and stay with even-money bets such as black or red. Increase your bet by one after losing, and decrease it by one after winning. You're favored to come out ahead in the end." He placed a chip on black.

She nodded and selected a ten-dollar chip for her first bet. The strategy sounded like him: smart, prudent, designed to minimize losses and maximize gains. But just as she was about to place the chip on the table, she drew her hand back. Then she swept all of her chips onto the number three.

"What are you doing?" His mouth hung slightly open. She'd never seen him look so nonplussed. Judging by the sideways glances thrown at him by the other players at their table, she wasn't the only one who thought his expression was unusual.

"I'm placing my bet."

He recovered his usual stoic expression. "I wouldn't advise it. The odds—"

"Yes. You told me. Thirty-eight to one."

The croupier dropped the ball into the spinning outer circle, a streaking silver blur.

"You can still change your mind," he said.

"Nope," she said. "I'm all in."

The ball began to fall from the rim and the croupier called, "No more bets."

Danica found herself crossing her fingers, and she relaxed them. Beside her, Luke's disapproval was evident in the rigid set of his shoulders and the straight line of his mouth.

But sometimes risks were worth taking. Her parents took a risk when they left their war-torn homeland. She took a risk, moving to California without knowing anyone. Taking on Luke's cockamamie search for a wife was the biggest risk of all. Certainly to her professional reputation, if word got out. But she wouldn't exchange her time with him for all the regular pay slips in the world.

She just had to remember not to risk anything else around him.

The ball flashed around the roulette wheel, clattering and clicking. Danica held her breath, waiting for the moment when the ball would drop into the slot—

"Three red. Odd," the croupier intoned. She left a marker by Danica's pile of chips and turned her attention to the rest of the table. After the croupier paid out the smaller bets, she began to add chips next to Danica's stack. And more. And still more. When the croupier was finished, Danica could build her own minifortress out of her winnings.

"What was the strategy you recommended?" she asked Luke as she raked the chips toward her, careless of their denominations. "I won, so I should bet one less chip this time?" She grinned up at Luke, catching his gaze.

It was a mistake. She thought he might be amused or perhaps annoyed she had gone against his advice. Instead, his gaze was warmly admiring, a bright glow shining in the dark blue depths. She nearly knocked a quarter of her chips onto the ground.

He probably used that expression with any female in his vicinity, she admonished herself sternly. He was Luke Dallas. He couldn't help it. Besides, he made it crystal clear this was a business outing.

Yet he'd looked at Felicity as if he couldn't wait for a polite reason to leave the party…

"That was bold," he said in his low rumble.

Danica wrenched her gaze away and began playing with a chip. "Nothing ventured, nothing gained, et cetera."

"You could have lost everything."

"Or I could've gained far more than I had before. Which I did."

"You got lucky," he said. "It paid off. But it was a—"

"I know the odds. But sometimes you have to put yourself in the hands of the universe."

"Fine when playing with fake money. But in real life? Not an advisable strategy."

She had the distinct impression they were no longer talking about casino games, but she didn't know if she was up to examining the undercurrents. She grabbed a five-hundred-dollar chip off the nearest pile. "Here. Go ahead, risk it all in one place," she said with a wide smile.

Luke took it from her, his gaze intent on hers. Their fingers brushed, electricity traveling the length of her arm and heading deep inside her. Instead of placing the chip down on the table, he tucked it into the inner pocket of his tuxedo jacket. Next to his heart. "Are you hungry?" he asked.

She was. For what, she couldn't quite put into words. She nodded, and Luke turned to the croupier. A few exchanged words later and Danica's mountain of round plastic circles had turned into a written receipt with nearly more zeros on it than space allowed. He handed it to her. "I'd repeat my advice not to risk it all in one place, but you might break the bank."

She folded up the receipt and placed it into her dress pocket. "No, you're right. I'd probably lose all my money on the next spin. That's what is exciting about it."

He tucked her hand into the crook of his elbow without looking. The automatic assumption she would go wherever he led would have rankled coming from anyone else. But with Luke, whose usual demeanor was closed off and forbidding, the gesture made her feel wanted, accepted. As if she belonged, now and forever.

He guided her toward the outdoor terrace, where different chefs from San Francisco's best restaurants had set up food stations. "Losing is exciting?"

She laughed. "No. It's terrifying. But sometimes, on a night like tonight… Don't you ever want to be surprised? Take a chance? Not know what's going to happen in advance?"

He shook his head. "I read the last pages of a book first."

She stopped walking, causing him to halt. "That's terrible."

"It's smart. I know I won't waste my time if the conclusion is unsatisfactory."

"What about serendipity?" *Like the serendipity of running into him outside Johanna's office?* "Or fate? Fortune?"

"Fate and fortune are excuses made by the unprepared. I know the odds and play them accordingly." He laced his words with authority, his mouth settling into a firm line when he finished speaking.

She slid a sideways glance in his direction. "Not everything in life can be controlled," she said softly.

He gave no indication he'd heard her, but she had to double her steps to keep up with him as he threaded his way through the crowd. She decided to relax and enjoy herself, creating mental snapshots as they sped through the party. She couldn't wait to tell Matt all about it during their next phone call. This beat any episode of *Real Housewives* they'd watched in Matt's hospital room.

Luke slowed down once they arrived on the stone terrace wrapping the length of the mansion. It was lined by long buffet tables, each one labeled with the name of one of San Francisco's most exclusive eateries. She tugged on his arm.

"Is that Shijo Nagao?" she asked, indicating a chef standing behind a station offering sushi prepared to order. Nagao's restaurant had a yearlong reservation waiting list.

Luke glanced over. "I believe so."

Danica dropped her hand from his sleeve. "See you later."

He grabbed her fingers. "You're ditching your work assignment? For raw fish?"

"Sushi," she corrected, allowing her hand to linger in his so she could enjoy the fizzy crackles his touch sent singing through her blood. "Expertly prepared, delicious raw fish. And omega-3 is vital to brain function. I'm sure you agree this would help me excel at my responsibilities." She flashed him a grin, daring him to find fault with her logic.

He narrowed his gaze. "What happened to the woman with the New England palate?"

"She likes fish."

"Fish served with wasabi. If you don't like salsa..."

She shuddered. "No wasabi. Never trust anything green and pasty."

He raised his eyebrows in horror, but his upturned mouth betrayed his amusement. "If I didn't have other reasons to trust your judgment, I would reconsider our relationship."

The word *relationship* sent shockwaves throughout her body. She shook her head at herself. He meant it in a professional sense. "How can you eat sushi with wasabi? It destroys the flavor," she said.

"What? No. It enhances it. It's a—"

"Let me guess. Chemical reaction." She raised a teasing eyebrow.

"Yep. Some pairings are proven by trial and time to be the only choice for each other."

"I bet if we ask Chef Nagao, he will tell you when

diners add extra wasabi to their meal, it is a sign they can't appreciate the chef's subtle flavors and shouldn't be served the best fish."

Luke swung his attention from Nagao's chef station and focused on her. "Really?"

She nodded. "The diner misses out by insisting on wasabi."

Guests began to pack the space where they stood. Luke stepped closer to her, his presence acting like a shield. The beginning of his five-o'clock shadow was making its appearance. "Misses out," he said, his gaze warm on hers.

Something fluttered in her stomach, and she couldn't attribute it to her lack of an evening meal. "Yes."

"By sticking to the preconceived pairing."

She wet her suddenly dry lips. "Yes."

His gaze fixed on her mouth. "If one were to, say, go in another direction, the result might be greater than anticipated?"

The event planners needed to do something about the number of people in the room. She was struggling to take a deep breath. "When it comes to sushi—"

"Or gambling, apparently."

A waiter tried to squeeze behind Danica. The hard edge of his tray jostled her right into Luke. Her hands flew up to brace herself. They landed square on Luke's chest.

His arms encircled her and kept her upright. "Are you okay?"

No. She was not. His chest was hard and muscled under the thin wool of his jacket and finely woven cotton of his shirt. His leather and citrus scent teased her nose. But she would have been able to laugh off the incident if it weren't for his gaze, deeply blue and full of concern. For her.

Sound faded. The laughter and conversation, the jazz trio playing in a nearby room—all hushed save for the pounding of her heart. His arms tightened around her, creating a cocoon outside which no one existed. His gaze changed, turned deeper, darker. Concern faded to awareness. Then flared into desire.

"Danica." She felt her name more than heard it, a deep rumble reverberating underneath her splayed hands.

Anticipation fizzed through her, headier than any alcoholic beverage. "Yes?" she whispered.

He raised his right hand and brushed a curl off her face, his thumb lingering on the curve of her cheek. Thankfully, he kept his left hand locked at her waist, keeping her upright when her legs would've failed her. "What were you saying about serendipity?"

"I welcome it," she managed to breathe. Luke Dallas was going to kiss her. And she wanted him to kiss her. Wanted it more than she'd ever wanted anything else. One more kiss for her memories. One more kiss to sweeten her dreams and warm her nights.

He smiled but it didn't reach his eyes. His gaze remained darkly intent, hot enough to leave scorch marks as it traveled the outline of her lips. She lifted her chin and tilted her mouth. Her lips parted. His hand tightened at her waist, pressing her closer—

"Dallas!" a man said from behind Luke. "Just the man we were hoping to see tonight."

The bubbly anticipation fled. The sounds of the party flooded back: the clink of the glasses, the hum of voices, the occasional well-bred laugh. Luke straightened up and let go of her waist. "To be continued," he said to her in a low voice. Then his expression changed to one she knew all too well from their first meeting.

The man came up and shook Luke's hand. He was tan and well over six feet tall, his custom-tailored tuxedo revealing a graceful, broad-shouldered physique most commonly seen in champion swimmers. His dark blond hair, streaked with the kind of highlights only constant exposure to the sun could provide, fell into his eyes. He looked like he'd be more at home on the cover of a surfing magazine, but she knew not to judge people by their looks. He was probably a brilliant programmer or a marketing genius.

"I'm Grayson," he said to her with a firm handshake and a slow, highly charming grin. Then he turned back to Luke. "Evan here thinks his start-up is not only a unicorn, it's a decacorn. I say he might be right. What do you say?"

"I say I haven't heard of Evan or his company before," Luke said. "But a ten-billion-dollar valuation? Pretty damn rare."

"I'd love to tell you more," Evan said. "We have a great opportunity for a partnership with Ruby Hawk's tech. Do you have a minute?"

"Thanks, but I have a prior commitment." Luke offered his arm to Danica. "If you'll excuse us?" he said to the men, his words polite but firm.

"Word is Ruby Hawk might miss its acquisition target date. You'll need good partners for your next venture," said Grayson.

"Want advice on your start-up? Never pay attention to valley gossip." Luke's tone was breezy, but under her loose grip his muscles tensed.

"That came from Cinco Jackson. But I'd still like to talk with you," Evan said.

Luke's arm turned to solid steel. Danica dropped her hand. "Why don't you three have a conversation? I'll save some sushi for you," she said to Luke.

"I promised you dinner." His gaze added, "And more."

"I can stand in line for my own food," she replied with a smile. In a tone pitched just for Luke's ear, she continued, "I'm curious what Jackson knows. If the real reason for our search leaked…"

Luke regarded her. "You're concerned."

She nodded, teeth worrying her lip.

"Don't be. I can handle whatever Jackson throws." He turned back to the two men. "Sorry. Maybe some other time. But as you see, I have far more attractive plans right now." He started to tug her away.

She saw a flash of navy blue silk from across the room. When she tried to catch Felicity's gaze, the other woman looked away, as if hoping to not get caught. "This is a charity event, right?" Danica asked. "And a key feature of this event is the auction?"

Three pairs of eyes focused on her. "Yes," Evan said slowly.

She opened her purse and pulled out the scrip given to her by the roulette croupier. "These are my winnings, which I planned to donate during the auction." She showed the total to Grayson and Evan. "I will let you have a half hour of my time with Luke if you each promise to match the amount."

"I wasn't aware I was up for sale," Luke said drily. She flicked her gaze upward, dreading to see the anger directed her way for selling him out. Instead, his gaze sizzled with appreciation. She flushed hot from her hairline to her big toe.

Grayson laughed. "You drive a hard bargain," he said. "But I agree. C'mon, Dallas, let's go find a place to talk. I don't want the other sharks milling about to hear about Evan's company. Not until we're ready, that is."

"Not so fast." She held out her hand. "Your checks, please."

"Smart *and* pretty," Grayson said to Luke. "You know how to pick them. Hope that goes for companies too." He pulled out his wallet and took out a business card. "Here. You bid on what you want during the auction, up to the combined amount Evan and I owe you. When you win, give this to the cashier and say I will pay the balance."

She took the card, raising a skeptical eyebrow. "Really—" she started to say, and then looked at the name. Grayson was Grayson Monk. As in Monk Partners, one of the top venture-capital firms in Silicon Valley. "I mean, really. You will."

Grayson clapped Luke on the shoulder. "Great. Now let's go make another deal."

"Fine," Luke said to the two men, but his gaze rested on Danica, that light still burning. "We'll talk mythical beasts. And even more mythical company valuations."

A large grin spread over Evan's face. "You won't regret it."

"Your five-hundred-dollar chip says I will," Luke muttered for Danica's ears only. His warm breath stirred the sensitive hairs there, sending a shiver through her. "Meet you back here when I'm done?" When she nodded, he turned back to the men. "A deal is a deal. You have thirty minutes."

Danica watched them walk away. Then she turned to get into the ever-growing line for Chef Nagao. Just as she reached the end, a man in a white dinner jacket thrust two empty champagne glasses at her. "Take these, will you?" he said, and turned his back on her. She accepted the glasses out of pure reflex, and then stared dumbfounded at his jacket-clad back.

What the...? She looked around for somewhere to put the flutes down, but no appropriate surfaces presented themselves. The low stone walls surrounding the terrace were roughhewn, the surface uneven. The high round cocktail tables dotting the outer sweep of the terrace were three deep in elegant people. She doubted they would appreciate dirty glassware set down beside their plates of beautifully prepared food. No busing station could be spotted in the vicinity.

Finally, she spotted a waitress carrying a silver tray overloaded with discarded china and glassware striding briskly through the throng and down the terrace steps to a flagstone walkway below. Danica hurried after her, catching up just as the waitress was about enter a white marquee tent set up behind a large, six-car detached garage.

"Here." Danica held out the empty flutes.

The waitress looked Danica up and down, her upper lip curling into a sneer. "Take them yourself," she said. "And where's your tray?" She disappeared behind a pinned-back flap.

If the guest handing her his empty flutes had been rude, the waitress was out of line. But it wasn't the waitress's exasperation that caused Danica to stare after her. It was her outfit. She sported a black dress almost identical to the one Danica wore. They even had on similar shoes.

It was official. She didn't belong at the party as a guest. Looking around the tent, she spotted a table full of dirty dishes. Quickly adding the flutes to the pile, she stepped out before anyone else could mistake her for a slack member of the catering team.

She returned to the terrace, but Chef Nagao's station had a Closed—Gone Fishing sign next to empty sushi display cases. Luke was nowhere in sight. When a woman wearing a gown Danica had seen in last month's *Vogue* approached her, empty plates in her hand and an annoyed scowl on her face, Danica ducked down the terrace steps again.

She should leave. She almost kissed Luke. Again.

She was playing with matches, testing how long she could hold on to the sliver of wood before burning her fingers. But if she snuck out now, then her gambling winnings plus Grayson's and Evan's pledges would not go to the charity. She had to stay until the auction started.

Might as well kill the time exploring one of the many gravel paths snaking through the mansion's expansive grounds. When would she get another chance to wander through a billionaire's backyard?

The path she chose meandered through formal gardens of well-manicured bushes and profusely blooming flower beds. Danica took notes of the varieties, knowing her mom would ask. At the end of the walkway was a wrought-iron garden bench, set in a small cul-de-sac formed by shoulder-high hedges.

It was hard to believe a party full of the Bay Area's brightest and wealthiest was being held a scant fifty yards away. She sat down to admire the evening. The sky overhead had deepened to indigo blue, decorated by a shining crescent moon. A light breeze carrying the scent of nearby roses ruffled strands of hair that had escaped from her ponytail. Later it would be too chilly to be outside without a jacket or sweater, but for now the temperature was perfect.

Gravel crunched on the other side of the hedge. She wasn't the only one to escape into the gardens. She stood up to return to the house but sat back down when she overheard Luke's name.

"He said what?" a male voice asked.

Danica frowned. The voice was familiar. "It wasn't Dallas. It was the recruiter," a female answered.

That voice Danica knew. Felicity. The male voice must belong to Cinco Jackson.

"You're missing the point. It's illegal to ask someone about their marital status in a job interview."

Danica's blood chilled.

Felicity protested from the other side of the hedge. "But the recruiter didn't ask. I was so surprised anyone knew, I confirmed it."

"You're still not seeing the point." Jackson spoke to her as if she were a small child. "Does Dallas have something against employing women who are married? Does he only employ single women? Is this a behavior pattern?"

Danica clasped her hands over her mouth. She needed to find Luke, quick. But if she left her bench now, the couple on the other side might hear her movements and know they had an eavesdropper.

"Something's up. I can smell it," Jackson continued. "The acquisition is rumored to be going south, maybe because old man Stavros has something on Dallas. Let's get back to the party." Rustling came from the other side as the hedges, as if they were standing up. "I want to see who Dallas is talking to and what about." The sound of gravel crunching underneath their feet drowned out anything else he said.

Danica waited until their footsteps faded away. Then she unfolded herself from the bench, scrambling for her phone to contact Luke. The screen already had a message on it.

Where are you? Sushi closed.

She thought for a moment. With the party in full swing and the auction about to start, the entrance would probably be the least occupied space in the mansion.

Meet you in the foyer. I have news.

Good I hope? See you there.

The crowd had grown exponentially in the time she had been gone. A few faces lit up when they saw her heading in their direction, but they turned dark as she pushed past without taking the dirty plates and used glasses they offered to her. It wasn't her fault the hosts didn't hire enough catering staff, even if she did accidentally crash the party dressed like a server.

She reached the foyer, slowing her speed so she wouldn't slide on the polished marble floor. Luke stood near the imposing double doors that led to the front drive and the valet station outside. He smiled, and the bands holding her lungs captive since she first overheard Cinco started to relax.

"Excuse me." Danica felt a hard tap on her shoulder. "You need to take this."

Danica turned her head to see the server who had scowled at her earlier. She held out a tray laden with empty champagne flutes, dirty dishes and crumbled napkins.

"Sorry," Danica said over her shoulder, picking up her pace again. "I'm not—"

The server followed behind her. "I have to be at the bar station. Your hands are free."

"I—you don't understand. I'm here as a—"

"I have to go, *now*. Here." The server thrust the tray at Danica.

Six

The tray left the server's hands. Danica lunged to catch it. Her thin-soled shoes slid, slipping on the smooth floor. Her feet flew out from underneath her. The last thing she saw before hitting the ground was the server's horrified face, her mouth in a perfect O.

Danica belly flopped on the marble floor. The impact knocked all her senses off-line. Black fog mired her thoughts. She concentrated on her breathing, thankful her heart beat by itself. Bells rang in the distance.

She wriggled her fingers to see if they worked. Good. Then she moved her left hand. A shard of glass sliced into her palm.

The sudden pain shocked her into full awareness. Her gaze swam back into focus, and she realized the bells were her ears ringing from the tray and its contents clattering down around her. She inhaled deeply. Then she wished she hadn't. It smelled like a liquor store had exploded around her.

"Danica!" Luke knelt beside her. Evan and Grayson stood behind him. She struggled to sit up.

"Wait," Luke warned. "Look at me. Did you hit your head?"

She stared into his gaze. His eyes were the color of the Pacific Ocean right before a thunderstorm. He was angry. And upset. For her? Or for the scene she'd caused?

"I'm fine." She broke the intense contact, giving Evan her uninjured hand so he could pull her upright.

Guests and members of the catering staff crowded into the space. The server stood nearby, wringing her hands. Danica shook her head at her, to indicate it wasn't her fault, and instantly wished she hadn't. Voices echoed off the surrounding marble, adding to her disorientation.

"I'm sorry—" she started to say to Luke, but her lips—her whole body—started to shake despite every effort to stop it.

He grabbed her hurt hand and examined it. "You're bleeding."

"It's just a scratch." She kept her gaze focused on his shoulder. The foyer was starting to tilt and the last thing she wanted to do was fall again.

"You need a doctor." He handed her the pocket square from his tuxedo jacket to press against her palm, and then threw an arm over her shoulder. It was comforting and solid, and she sank into his side. "We're leaving."

"But the auction—"

"Don't worry about the auction," Grayson said from her other side. "I'll make sure all the money gets to the charity."

Danica started to thank him, but the heavy wooden doors had opened and she was standing in the cool evening air before she knew it. The valet had Luke's car ready and Luke opened the passenger door, guiding her in.

She slid onto the smooth leather seat and buckled in, careful to keep her injured palm from touching anything, and closed her eyes to stop the last of the spinning. The car accelerated and she opened them to see Luke, his expression grim in the glow of the car's display.

"The closest emergency room is twenty minutes away. You'll be okay until then?" His words were clipped.

She took her head off the pillow-like headrest and sat upright. "Do you know how expensive a trip to the ER is? If you drop me off at the nearest Caltrain station, I'll be able to get home."

"Don't worry about money. Your hand needs to be looked at. And what if you hit your head?"

She took the pocket square off her palm and looked at the cut in the dim light. "I think the bleeding has stopped. And I know I didn't hit my head. I don't need a doctor." Thanks to Matt, she'd had enough of hospitals to last her several lifetimes.

He made a sound in his throat like he didn't believe her. Then he turned the car around in a smooth, tight arc.

"What are you doing? Are we going back to the party?"

"I live a few streets away," he answered. "If you won't see a doctor, the least I can do is make sure your hand is cleaned and bandaged."

"But—"

"I'm not taking no for an answer."

She opened her mouth to insist otherwise, but he cut her off.

"I mean it," he said tightly. "Hang on, we'll be there soon."

She opened her mouth again.

"Don't even try."

She pressed her lips together. He was being ridiculous. She was fine. Well, except for her heart rate beating in triple time. It was quiet in the car and dark, and they sat close enough that she could extend her hand just an inch or two and touch his thigh.

She barely lost any blood. She shouldn't feel this faint.

In what seemed like no time, he swung the car off the road. They passed a sleek iron gate that opened automatically as they approached, and continued up a long, winding driveway that led to a two-story house set among pine trees and cypresses. It resembled a gray concrete box with steel trim, but natural-wood window frames and doors softened the hard materials and made the house feel more welcoming than imposing. Not a bad metaphor for Luke, she thought. Hard and masculine but there was warmth if you looked.

He opened her car door and ushered her into the house. "Go straight and make yourself at home in the living room," he said. "I'll get the first-aid kit."

She nodded, not trusting her voice, and walked down a short hallway into a wide room shaped like a rectangle. The house she rented with Mai could fit in it, with room for their next-door neighbor.

The far wall was clear glass, floor to ceiling, allowing her to see the dimly lit patio and gardens just beyond. It took her a second before she realized the wall was composed of retractable panels. When the weather was nice, Luke could open the panels and the room would flow into the outdoors without interruption. To her right was the kitchen, all polished stainless appliances and warm wooden veneers, separated from the rest of the room by low counters. A metal dining table surrounded by twelve mismatched chairs stood nearby.

To her left, a fireplace tall enough to stand up in dominated the wall. Arranged in front of it were two oversize, cream-colored leather sofas and several comfortable-looking chairs. A plush rug resembling a soft cloud that had landed on the floor completed the look, straight out of a pricey interior-design magazine.

The plump cushions beckoned her to sit down, but she hesitated. Her dress had soaked up several varieties of wine and other alcohol. Last thing she wanted to do was mar his pristine furniture.

"Pick a sofa," Luke said from behind her. His jacket and black bow tie had been discarded, and the top buttons of his crisp white shirt were undone, exposing a triangle of tanned skin. In his hands he held a white box marked with a red cross.

She indicated her stained dress. "The kitchen would be better."

He shook his head and steered her until she sank down onto cushions that were even softer than they looked. Her face must have shown her reaction because he smiled. "Much better than the kitchen. Now, give me your hand."

She extended it, managing to keep the trembling to a minimum. Just as she had informed him in the car, the bleeding had slowed. He took out a bottle of hydrogen peroxide and swabbed the area with gentle, sure movements. She reflexively tried to pull her hand back but he held on, his grip secure and firm.

Her pulse beat in her ears, a rapid flutter. She told herself it was a natural reaction to the sting of hydrogen peroxide hitting the wound. But then he traced his index finger over her palm and she knew her reaction had nothing to do with pain and everything to do with him.

She inhaled, her lungs requiring more air than she could take in. She couldn't remember the last time anyone took care of her. Oh, her parents had bandaged her childhood scrapes and put ointment on her bruises. But as soon as she was old enough to fend for herself, it became a point of pride to cause them as little concern as possible. Between trying to earn enough money to keep a roof over their heads and food on the table and looking after the energetic, never-met-a-dare-he-didn't-take Matt, her parents had enough worries.

She had been more often the caregiver than not, from babysitting her brother after school while her parents were still at work, to doing everything she could to help her college boyfriend ace the LSATs and apply to law school. Tom did get into a top program, thanks to her coaching. Then he attended law-school orientation, announced he had found the woman of his dreams among his fellow first-year students and dumped Danica.

"You can only rely on yourself and family," her father had said when she was still crawling into her childhood bed to cry under the covers three weeks later. When her boss at the time mentioned he knew an executive-recruitment firm in Palo Alto that needed an assistant, she took the money she had saved for a security deposit on an apartment with her now ex-boyfriend and spent it on a plane ticket to California. It was the furthest possible point from Tom and still in the continental United States. She would show everyone she could do just fine on her own.

But with Luke's touch trailing embers in its wake, it felt good to have someone look after her. More than good. A heaviness gathered deep and low, a persistent ache demanding to be relieved that she hadn't felt—well, she hadn't felt since Luke kissed her outside the taqueria in San Francisco. And before that, a very long time.

He took out a gauze pad and sterile tape. "You

weren't planning on using your hand much tonight, were you?"

"Um." Good thing it was her left hand, and she was right-handed. She definitely planned on using her right hand later that night while indulging in fantasies. Involving him. "No."

He bent his head down as he worked. It was all she could do to stop her mind from conjuring those fantasies, right here, right now. For example, what would happen if she leaned forward and pressed her lips to his? Would he welcome her kiss, without the music and the bright lights and the buzz of the party creating an alternate reality in which they moved in the same social world?

What would he taste like? Champagne, bright and tart? Or—

Snap out of it, Novak. She didn't belong here, sitting on a sofa that probably cost more than six months of her salary as Johanna's assistant, just as she didn't belong at that party where she barely passed for a guest. She certainly didn't belong in Luke Dallas's arms.

"You don't have to do this," she blurted out.

He finished bandaging her hand, smoothing the tape over the gauze with deliberate strokes of his fingers. Strokes that advanced and withdrew, creating an answering drumbeat rhythm between her legs. "Due diligence," he said with a half smirk, his gaze locked on hers as his fingers continued their caresses. "If the cut gets infected and you can't work, you could sue. A lawsuit might bankrupt the Peninsula Society."

"Oh." The pleasure-pain tightening deep in her belly

at the thought of kissing Luke lessened, just a bit. Then his smile deepened, and it roared back. She swallowed her own smile. "Well, we can't have that, can we," she said primly.

"Just controlling outcomes," he agreed, his gaze sparking with humor. Crinkles appeared at the corners of his summer-sea blue eyes.

A teasing Luke was catnip to her libido. She tugged her hand. He frowned but let it go. "Thank you for the bandage. I'll order a car to go home."

He sat back on the couch, his gaze never leaving hers. "What did you want earlier?"

"What?" She wasn't that transparent. Was she? She didn't need to touch her cheeks to know they were burning.

"Before your accident. You said you had news?"

The conversation in the garden felt like a lifetime ago. "Right." Clearing her throat, she forced herself to sound businesslike. "I overheard Cinco and Felicity." She filled him in on the details.

He made a noncommittal noise. "We knew he was nosing around Ruby Hawk."

"But this sounded personal," she said. "He thinks the acquisition is in trouble because Stavros has dirt on you."

"He's not wrong." Luke shrugged. "Nestor is refusing to close the deal until I meet his conditions. But I don't hire my employees based on marital status. If that's the tree Jackson wants to bark up, he'll be hoarse."

She released her breath. "So, what's the next step?"

His gaze traveled to the top of her head. "Take down your ponytail."

Her uninjured hand flew up to protect her hair. "What? Why?"

He leaned toward her, filling the space between them until only a handbreadth remained. "To see if you have any lumps resulting from hitting your head."

She searched his gaze. "I didn't hit my head."

"You were stunned after the accident so you might not be aware if you did or not. Let me check." His lips pressed together in a firm line.

"I'm capable of seeking my own medical attention," she warned.

"I know you're very capable," he said with a rueful smile. He leaned even closer. "Humor me. Please." His low rumble sent a cascade of goose bumps down her spine.

Perhaps he should check. The room was spinning again. "Fine," she agreed with an exhaled breath. Before she could finish speaking, his right hand reached behind her and removed the elastic holding her hair. Her curls tumbled around her face and bounced off her shoulders.

Intellectually, having her hair down should make her feel more covered up, hidden. Instead, it was as if he had stripped her of her armor, leaving her bare to his knowing gaze. She shivered.

His fingers combed through her hair, tracing small circles on her scalp. He was so close she could see the faint shadow of whiskers making their presence known along the strong line of his jaw, and the dusting of crisp black hairs revealed by the open throat of his shirt. Delicious awareness pricked to life. She leaned into his hands as if she were a cat.

He slowed and then stopped his movements, his fingers still tangled in her hair. "No lumps." His eyes were indigo dark, and the coiled tension she could sense reminded her again of a tiger, ready to pounce on its prey.

She very much wanted to be devoured. All she had to do was lean forward, just an inch, and her mouth would be on his.

"Was that the outcome you desired?" Somehow, she was able to form words.

"It was one," he growled.

"There was another?"

His gaze flared with a primal hunger, and his grasp tightened on her curls. "Only if you desire it, as well."

The air crackled with electricity. She could almost see golden sparks leaping between them, illuminating the thread of attraction that wove around them. She lifted her hand to cover his, encircling his wrist. Under her touch, his pulse beat in time with hers.

She should thank him for the medical attention, spring to her feet, find her phone and summon a ride-sharing service to take her home. That's what the old Danica would do. The one who worked long hours for Johanna, expecting a promotion that never came. The one who would have listened to Luke's explanation of how to maximize her roulette bets.

Or she could go all in. Risk everything. The Danica who piled all her chips on one number and waited for the ball to drop. The Danica who kissed Luke Dallas and was about to kiss him again.

Just one night. Not a relationship. It could never be a relationship. She knew where she stood with him. So, what would be the harm of giving in to the anticipation curling in her stomach, the throbbing emptiness between her legs demanding to be filled?

She took a deep breath. Her lips were dry, and she wet them with her tongue. His gaze followed its path. His blue eyes were almost black now. She closed the tiny gap between them and pressed her mouth against his.

Luke's history with women was long and varied. He liked sex, and the women he dated indicated they enjoyed having sex with him. But the players knew the cards on the table, making the stakes for all low. He never got involved unless the other party agreed to mutually assured pleasure and fun, nothing more. Still, there were plenty of women who were happy to share his bed on those terms.

Therefore, he thought he knew every variation on a kiss. The gentle kiss, the rough kiss. The soft slide of lip against lip and the thrusting duel of tongues. The nibble, the suck, the grind, the bite.

Then Danica kissed him. And he knew he had missed out on kissing all these years.

Kissing her was a shot of pure adrenaline, a narcotic hit to his system no manufactured drug could ever hope to match. It acted like a rocket booster, taking what had been a very pleasurable activity and sending it into the stratosphere. A pure jolt of electricity traveled straight from where their mouths met to his cock. He was rock hard in half a second.

His fingers tangled in those glorious blond curls. He loved the infinite variety of golds in its strands. It was as soft and yet as wildly dimensional as he thought it would be—alive to the touch.

Seeing her still on the ground, eyes closed, had shut his throat with fear. He may have used protecting the charity from lawsuits as an excuse to take care of her, but it was as transparent as the walls in his office. He'd needed, on some primal level he still hadn't fully acknowledged, to ensure she wasn't hurt.

And now he needed to kiss her senseless.

Her mouth was hot and insistent and greedy. He met her demands with his own, their tongues tangling and exploring. The scant millimeters separating them on the sofa felt like miles, and he gathered Danica to him, pulling her until she half lay across his lap. Her scent, vanilla and cinnamon, sweet and spicy, surrounded him. She shifted even closer, the curve of her bottom just brushing his groin. An involuntary shudder ran through to his toes, shocking his brain back to a limited cognitive function.

He should stop. She was his consultant. Her job was to find him a wife. A wife in every sense of the word. If all went to plan, he would be in front of a judge with another woman in a matter of weeks.

He couldn't stop even if a 7.8 earthquake hit the Bay Area that instant.

Her hands reached out to tug his shirt free from his

pants and moved up to work the buttons of his shirt free. The brush of her fingers against his chest brought his cock to a whole different level of density.

Turnabout was fair play. He undid the buttons on her shirtdress from throat to waist. Her skin was smooth, warm. He disengaged from her mouth so he could press his lips to where her neck joined her shoulder, inhaling her vanilla-cinnamon scent. He had to see if she tasted as good as she smelled, and he kissed-licked a path across her collarbone to where the dress gaped open. He pushed the top of the dress down, exposing high, full breasts straining against a cotton bra.

He trailed his right index finger over the generous swells, dipped it into the shadowy crevice between. Hard nipples pushed against the bra cups and with his thumbs he traced slow, tiny circles around each one.

"Luke," she breathed and tugged on his hair. He looked up to catch her gaze, wide and wild and dark. "You're still wearing your shirt."

He grinned. "I'm much more interested in removing yours." He kissed her again, his hands busy untying the sash at her waist then removing all the buttons he could find from their buttonholes, until her dress parted in the middle.

She really was beautiful. He shook his head in silent admiration and ran his index finger from the shadowy valley between her breasts to the top of her plain white panties. She shivered and gasped, her eyes squeezed shut.

"Are you cold?" he asked. He wasn't. He was burning up.

She shook her head, but when he undid the clasp of her bra, her hands came up to cross over her chest. "Wait. Before the rest comes off, I think we need to negotiate," she said, her words coming in bursts between gulps of air.

Those deep breaths caused her breasts to rise and fall, the fabric of her bra slipping even as she tried to hold it in place. It took a moment for him to realize she was speaking. "Negotiate?"

"Set boundaries, then. This is just for tonight. Nothing will change," she said. "Right?"

It was hard to think since all his blood had rushed south, but he managed to nod. "Of course."

She searched his gaze for a moment, her lower lip caught by her upper teeth. Then she nodded. "Of course." She stood up and let her arms drop, her bra falling with them. Her breasts were two perfect orbs custom-made to fill his hands. "This is comfy, but wouldn't a bed be preferable?"

Before a coherent thought could form, he was off the sofa. Leading her by the hand, he guided her to his bedroom.

"Put your hands on the bed," he breathed in her ear, and from behind his knee moved between her legs until she stood with them a shoulder's width apart. Then his hands stroked her thighs, starting above her knees and moving higher. His fingers found the waist of her panties, then slipped down farther, into the nest of soft curls.

She bucked against him, her perfect, round ass grinding against his painful erection. His breathing was harsh in his own ears as he found her opening and slid one finger, then two, slowly, deeply inside the wetness.

She gasped, then moaned. It was the sweetest sound he'd ever heard. There was nothing practiced about her response, no artifice or putting on a show. His thumb brushed the tight knot of nerves at the top of her opening—firm, then soft, then firm again—and her gasps came in short, quick bursts. "Luke," she breathed. "I need—"

"I know," he said, because he felt it too. She shuddered and tried to turn to face him.

He held her hips still. "Not yet," he said in her ear. Then he removed her panties and fell to his knees, his mouth closing over her sweet, hot core. Her taste was more exquisite than any food on offer at the party.

"What are you—" she squeaked out, before her words turned into a moan, low and full throated. The primal sound urged him on, harder, faster, deeper. He couldn't get enough. She was a white-hot flame and he yearned to be burned like he'd never been burned before. He could feel her tremble, her climax beginning to build, and he pulled back just in time to witness her scream and shudder before she collapsed against the bed.

He joined her on the king-size mattress, his erection pressing painfully against his tuxedo trousers, and turned her over. Her big green eyes flew open, dark with satisfaction. He grinned down at her. She was gorgeous, although the word was too inadequate to describe the sight before him. Who knew underneath her ponytail and always-appropriate work attire was such a responsive, passionate woman? *You knew. Since the moment you kissed her. You knew she was special.*

"That was…" she breathed, her chest still rising and falling rapidly. "Can't think." He watched her gaze slowly focus. "You. Too many clothes. Take them off."

Her hands reached out, her fingers still trembling, and she tugged his shirt open. At least one button, torn free from its mooring, clattered on the hardwood floor, but he didn't care. He needed to feel her skin against his. Then her hands moved lower and caressed him through his trousers, causing him to buck like a teenager in the back seat of a car. "Inside," she breathed. "Want you inside."

He didn't have to be asked twice. The rest of his clothes came off even faster than he could open the foil packet and avail himself of the contents. Her eyes widened when she saw him revealed for the first time, but her lips curved upward in a wide smile as she opened her arms to him.

He couldn't wait any longer. He had to have her. Not even as a teenager had he felt so excited yet anxious with anticipation. She was so responsive. So alive and present. He slid into her, closing his eyes and biting back a moan at the slick, tight heat.

His control was legendary. He should have no problem holding out. But the rake of her fingers on his back inflamed his senses, her gasps urging him to go faster, deeper. The pressure built, more rapidly than he thought possible. It demanded to be brought to its inescapable conclusion, now. He gritted his teeth. He

was not an inexperienced boy with his first girlfriend.
But then she cried out underneath him, her vibrations
shaking the bed.

Stars exploded behind his eyelids.

When he had recovered, he gathered her limp, pli-
ant body to his, pressing a kiss to the soft dusting of
freckles across her nose. She blinked and looked up at
him, a lazy smile playing on her lips. "Best outcome
to a negotiation I've ever had," she said.

Male pride expanded his chest. He pulled her closer,
burying his face in those curls. Cinnamon and vanilla
surrounded him, a combination sweet yet warm and
spicy. Just like her.

She sighed, her body fitting against his without any
awkwardness as she fell into slumber. None of the unexpected sharp elbow or accidental knee to the groin
that often occurred on a first night together. He could
stay like this forever, he thought as he drifted into the
kind of sleep that came only after truly satisfying sex.

Then his eyes flew open.

Forever?

What kind of a thought was that?

Sex was of the moment, experienced in the here and
now. Relationships could be mutually beneficial but
like most partnerships, they needed to be periodically
assessed and reconfigured. Look at his parents. Their
marriage lasted five years, enough time to produce him
and his younger sister. His father, Jonathan, got entry
into the San Francisco society that had previously rejected him for having more money than manners, while
his mother, Phoebe, secured access to the Dallas for-

tune for the rest of her children's lifetimes. Each of his parents' subsequent marriages had further enhanced their financial standing, social standing or both.

Luke raised himself on his elbow to gaze at the woman curled into his side. She wouldn't enhance his family's social status or their bank accounts. She was...

She was Danica.

He fell asleep with her name branded on his thoughts.

Someone shook Luke's shoulder, soft but insistent. "Hey."

He opened his eyes to find Danica standing over him. She was dressed, her black shirtdress somewhat rumpled but buttoned to her collarbone. He pushed himself up on one elbow, but she started to speak before he could form coherent thoughts.

"Hi. Sorry to wake you. But I'm going home." Her gaze didn't meet his. It swept the floor as if searching for something. Suddenly she bent down. When she came back up into his field of vision, he recognized the white cotton panties in her right hand. She thrust them into her dress pocket. In her other hand, she held her cell phone.

He blinked, still struggling to make his synapses fire. "You don't have to—"

"Yes, I do," she said firmly, then chased it with a quick smile her eyes didn't reflect. "Lot of work tomorrow. We both need sleep."

"We were sleeping." He stretched out a hand. "Come back to bed."

She stepped out of his reach. "I only wanted to tell you I was leaving."

"What's wrong?" It couldn't be the sex. No, the sex had been amazing. Mind-blowing. Call him arrogant or just experienced at these things, but he knew she'd enjoyed herself. Twice.

She laughed, two octaves higher than her normal range. "Everything is fine. I only woke you up because it wouldn't be right to sneak out. I mean, you're still my client and I still owe you work. Right?"

"Right." He searched her gaze. She wasn't telling the complete truth. He could sense it. But he never fought to keep a woman in his bed. If she wanted to leave, that was her choice.

He pushed down the unexpected wave of emotion. No, he wasn't disappointed. How could he be? This was the best possible outcome: great sex then his partner leaves. No morning awkwardness, no worrying if she will expect breakfast and especially no verbal dance around the possibility of an encore.

He swung the covers off. "I'll drive you."

"No!" She averted her gaze from his nude torso. "I called a car. You don't need to bother."

"It's not a—"

"Look!" She thrust her phone at him. "My driver is almost here. Silver Corolla. Can't cancel now. It would be rude." She lowered the phone but kept her gaze riveted on its screen. "So, um, thanks for the party. And the…rest. I had a good time. I mean, I hope you had a good time. No, I mean—"

"Danica." He waited until she looked up and held his gaze. A deep line still creased her brow.

He wanted to sweep the curls off her face and tell her everything would be okay. He wanted to hold her curves against him and caress that soft skin until she agreed to crawl back under the covers.

Wait. That was wrong. He didn't want bed partners to stay. He masked his confusion with a tight smile. "I had a great time. Thank you."

Her shoulders descended. "So, I'll see you in the morning? At Ruby Hawk?"

"Of course."

"Business as usual?"

"Yes." Good. They were each appropriately categorizing the evening as a fun, one-time experience. The sour, hollow feeling in his stomach must be hunger from skipping dinner at the party.

Her phone buzzed. She glanced down at the screen. "The driver is outside the gate." She took a step toward the bed, but when he reached out his arm to draw her close for a goodbye kiss, she retreated to the doorway and offered a wave of her hand instead. "Bye."

And she was gone.

He leaned back against the pillows. The bed held her smell, the air quivered with her presence. He waited for the room to settle and return to being his. Still. Quiet. Orderly. He twitched the sheets back into place and punched the pillows into perfect fluffed form. The room was back to status quo, and so was he.

When he woke again, hours before his alarm was set to ring, he was clasping the pillow she'd used tight to his chest. He tried his usual methods for dropping back into sleep, but none of them worked.

There was only one thing to do: diagram the situation causing his insomnia and diagnose the solutions. By the time he stepped into the shower to begin his work day, he'd made three key decisions.

Number one: the search was off. Danica was careful, but the odds had changed. With Cinco Jackson sniffing around, the search was no longer a calculated risk in his favor. He needed Nestor to believe the marriage commitment was real. A front-page story about his pursuit of unmarried females would call that into question.

Number two: he still needed a wife.

Number three: the only logical solution to his dilemma was Danica.

Seven

Luke pushed open the glass doors of Ruby Hawk, eager to put his plan into action. He had examined it from all angles in the hours before the sun rose, not finding a single flaw. And after discovering just how combustible they were in bed, Danica would agree with him, of course.

"You seem chipper," Anjuli said when she ran into him at the coffee bar. "That's not your usual style the morning after the Peninsula Society shindig. Did you not go?"

"I went. Have you heard of Medevco?"

Anjuli raised an eyebrow at the sudden change of subject. "Is that a city or a company?"

"Company. High-tech medical devices."

She shook her head. "No, but I haven't been following the health-care sector too closely."

"Check it out, would you? Evan Fletcher is the founder. Grayson Monk is the key investor." He saluted her with his three-shot Americano. He needed to get some work done before he took Danica to lunch to explain his stroke of genius. In fact, perhaps he should clear his schedule for the rest of the day. Just in case. The hot flare of anticipation at the thought was not unwelcome.

He frowned as he approached the conference room he used as his office. The mechanized shades were down, turning the glass walls opaque. He was positive he had left them up. With all the rumors surrounding Ruby Hawk, it was important to project openness and confidence. He opened the door.

And immediately wished he hadn't.

Irene Stavros sat behind his desk, thumbing through that blasted *Silicon Valley Weekly*. "Hello," she greeted him. "I'm so sorry I missed you at the fund-raiser last night. But it looks like you had a great time despite my absence." She turned the paper around so he could see the double-page spread. A photo of him and Danica talking to Grayson Monk occupied the center. Her manicured fingernail tapped on Danica's face. "What I can't figure out is why you were seen leaving with the help."

What did I do? What did I do? What did I do? The refrain would not stop playing in Danica's mind. She fell asleep listening to its rhythmic beat, and the words provided the background soundtrack for her shower, breakfast and now her journey to work. She barely noticed the scenery as she walked the six blocks from the train station to the Ruby Hawk offices. Images and sounds and scents from the night before occupied her senses.

She slept with Luke Dallas.

No. Strike that.

She had sex with Luke Dallas. Mind-blowing, can't-see-straight, volcanic sex. The kind magazines wrote headlines about. The kind appearing in books she previously filed under fantasy.

That she and Luke had chemistry had been obvious since that first kiss outside the taqueria. But even very, very, *very* good sex wasn't enough to ruin her career over. This…whatever it was…could go no further.

And Luke was sure to agree. After all, he hired her to find him a wife, and she wasn't on the list. Last night was impulsive madness, fueled by champagne and pent-up curiosity.

Now they knew. It was over and done. There wouldn't be a repeat.

Autopilot brought her to the converted supply room that was her office. Taking a deep breath, she sat down behind her desk and wrote down her game plan. She would find Luke the third candidate, she would submit her invoice for a job completed and then she would leave Ruby Hawk and start her own search firm.

Her phone dinged with a text message. Her mom.

Please call when you can? Bank refuses to refinance mortgage but drs. say Matt needs 6 more months minimum of physical therapy. Would like your help to decide if we should sell the house. Love you.

"I'm glad you're here." A deep male voice interrupted her text reading. A very familiar voice.

Luke leaned against her doorway with his arms folded across his chest. It was all she could do to stop herself from staring at how the cloth skimmed and outlined his muscles.

She tore her gaze away to focus on her computer. "It's nine thirty. I'm obscenely early judging by the hours some of your programmers keep." She hit a few keys. She had no idea which ones. Her concentration was shot between the message from her mother and Luke's presence. "Do you need something?"

He unfolded himself from the doorway and walked to her desk until he stood before it. "Just you."

What the— She whipped her head up, thoughts bouncing around at the speed of light. Had he hit his head sometime between now and last night? Was he on drugs? Had he been replaced by a robot with the wrong programming? Before she could come up with another explanation, his long fingers tilted her face farther up. Then his lips closed over hers.

Shock caused her to remain still. And then the electricity that always arced between them took over, opening her mouth wide in welcome, tangling and sliding her tongue against his. Warmth began to tug deep in her belly and pool between her legs. She heard a squeak of a moan and realized it came from her. She couldn't pull away from him if she tried.

She didn't want to try.

He broke contact first. "Good morning. I didn't get a chance to say it earlier." His gaze burned with want. But his mouth was set in a firm line, and tension held his shoulders straight.

"Morning," she stammered, gathering her thoughts from where they had flown into the ionosphere. "What brought—"

He shook his head slightly, as if in warning. "I want to introduce you to someone. An old friend. I don't think you've met." He straightened up and stepped back, and Danica realized there was a woman standing in her doorway. She barely had time to process her expensive haircut and her impeccable designer outfit when Luke spoke. "Danica, meet Irene Stavros. We went to business school together. Irene, meet Danica. My wife."

His…*what?* Danica stared at him as he sat on a corner of her desk. Nor did she resist when he picked up her left hand and held it firmly in his. She'd heard him wrong. Right?

One glance at Irene and Danica knew, no, she had indeed heard him correctly. Irene's face was smoothly noncommittal, but Danica's experience as an executive recruiter meant she was rather good at reading others. Irene vibrated with curiosity.

Luke, what are you doing? Danica tugged her left hand free and stood up, offering Irene her right to shake. "Nice to meet you. I've heard a lot about you." The latter was not a lie.

Irene's handshake was firm, almost bruising. "Charmed," she said. "I wish I could say the same about you. But this bad boy here never said a word. You kept this very quiet, Luke," she chided lightly.

"Oh, well, you know," Danica said with a shrug, hoping to appear nonchalant on the surface. "We're quiet types." Underneath, a bubbling mixture of disbelief, anger and shock twisted and roiled. Besides, what else could she say? She didn't know what Luke had told Irene or why Luke came up with such a preposterous story in the first place. What she did know is she didn't like the amused glint in Irene's gaze as it travelled from the top of Danica's ponytail to her practical low-heeled pumps.

"No, I'm afraid I don't know," Irene said after she finished her visual inspection, with a smile bordering on a smirk. "You're not even wearing a ring. You must tell me sometime how this whirlwind marriage came to be. Perhaps lunch? Are you free?"

"No," Luke said firmly. "She's having lunch with me. Sorry, but the reservation is only for two. You understand."

"Mmm-hmm." Irene continued to regard Danica with a mixture of appraisal and mirth. "And restaurants never allow reservations to be changed, of course."

Danica unfolded the arms she had been hugging to her chest. For a second, she was back in middle school, her thrift-shop dress and unruly curls the target of girls with shining straight hair and the latest fashions from the mall.

Then she remembered she had weapons of her own.

"Sure," she said. "Come to lunch with us." She picked up Luke's hand and pressed a kiss into his palm. "It would be fun, right, honey?"

His fingers tightened on hers. "I was looking forward to having you all to myself," he rumbled, tilting her chin up so he could press a kiss on her lips. "Irene reminded me we need to pick up our rings."

She was pretty sure he kissed her just to hide his smirk, but she kissed him back anyway, her eyes fluttering closed, before she remembered it was just playacting. "We have plenty of time for that. Wouldn't it be fun getting to know Irene better?" She beamed at the other woman.

"You two are just so adorable," Irene said, her expression still amused. But her smile no longer met her eyes. "I'd be delighted—" A shrill buzz cut off her words. She dug into her Hermès Kelly bag and brought out a sleek new phone. "It looks like I won't be free for lunch anyway. Duty calls." She looked up from the device. "My father can't wait to meet Veronica."

"Danica," Luke said.

"Right." Irene typed the name into her phone. She pulled a business card out of her purse and handed it to Danica. "Do call me. I'd love to throw you a party to celebrate the happy occasion. Don't worry, it will be a small gathering. But there are some people I'm sure you're not acquainted with that you really must know."

She smiled a perfect smile of perfect teeth surrounded by perfect red lips.

Danica was abruptly reminded she didn't put on makeup that morning. Still, she returned Irene's expression, bared incisor for bared incisor. "Sounds delightful," she gushed.

"Great! In the meantime, I'll send Luke the details of my stylist. Just in case you don't have your own." Her bright gaze lingered on Danica's blouse, bought on clearance several years ago at a discount store. "But now, I better run. So nice seeing you, Luke. Congratulations, again. Danica, lovely to meet you. Talk to you soon." She waved, a slight bending of fingers at the tips, and left the cramped office.

Danica waited until Irene disappeared. Then she went to the door and peered down the hallway.

"She's gone," Luke said.

"I wasn't looking for her," Danica said, shutting the door and whirling on the balls of her feet to face Luke. "I wanted to make sure no one could hear me yell at you." Her pulse beat in her throat, threatening to close off her airways. "I may have slept with you last night, but that doesn't give you permission to pull me into your game with Irene!"

Luke took a step toward her, his hands held out. "Danica—"

"Don't come closer," she warned. The last thing she needed was to be overcome by Luke's nearness. Or for him to kiss her again. She was angry, damn it, and she had the right to be angry.

"I know you're upset," Luke began.

"Understatement of the century. Try furious, livid, rage filled—"

He held up a hand. "And you deserve to be. But think about it. It's a win-win."

She scoffed. "This may come as a shock, but every woman who sleeps with you doesn't automatically want to marry you."

Despite her warning, he took two steps toward her.

She moved backward until her rear end hit the door. She took comfort from the solid material. She could be just as unyielding. If she tried.

"Think about it," he said. "It's the right solution to the search."

"Luke—" she warned.

"I know you're not happy with me."

"Again, understatement of the century."

A ghost of a smile momentarily creased his face. "The century is still relatively young. I can live with that."

Despite everything, her lips quirked upward.

"And we kill whatever story Cinco Jackson is planning," he continued.

She frowned. "Marrying your search consultant doesn't put out that fire. On the contrary."

"How can I look at other women when I have you in my life?" A spark lit deep in his gaze.

It was amusement. It had to be. But for a brief second, Danica imagined what it would be like if his words were the truth. If she mattered to his life, was the center of his focus. She swallowed, hard, and looked away. "What's the other win?"

"You fulfill the terms of your contract. Before the deadline, so you qualify for the bonus."

"Bonus?"

He held up three fingers and counted them down as he spoke. "Jayne, Felicity and you. That makes three candidates I've accepted."

"But I'm not a candidate." She laughed. It was either that or cry. "Last night was…last night. I wanted to be there. It wasn't an audition. I don't meet the criteria."

"You think fast on your feet, you handled the Felicity situation with grace under pressure, and I received a thank-you this morning from the Peninsula Society. Grayson Monk gave a very generous donation. He credited you for daring him to match your winnings at the roulette table." He moved a step closer, his blue gaze frank and warm. "You more than fulfill the requirements."

Every cell in her body ached to believe him. Then she remembered he was a skilled negotiator, while she was tired, worried for her family and still on sensory overload from the night before.

She shook her head. "I can't be part of a pretend marriage."

"Who said anything about pretending?"

She blinked rapidly, trying to parse his meaning. "Of course we'd be pretending."

"No. We'll be married. As soon as possible."

He spoke in English, but his words didn't make sense. "Married? Like, *married* married?"

"If by married married you mean legally, then yes."

"Married…in every sense of the word?"

His gaze fell to her chest. Her nipples tightened at the visible appreciation in his eyes. "That would be an advantage of this deal."

Would it ever... Wait. He was far too sure of himself. "Again, just because I slept with you once, it does not mean I want to repeat it, much less be legally tied to you."

The hot light left his gaze. He ran his right hand through his hair, leaving it mussed. Just like it looked when she'd stood by his bed and said goodbye. "I know our association started to save the acquisition. And I still need to present a wife to Nestor Stavros."

"I'm your recruiter." Even as she said the words, a memory flash of how he'd caused her to scream his name turned her cheeks to flame. "We agreed last night would not affect our business relationship."

He moved closer. There was a slight bite mark just below his jaw. She could still taste his skin, the rasp of his whiskers stinging her tongue. If she just leaned forward, she could kiss that reddened area better...or do more damage.

Right now, she was torn.

"We would still have a business relationship. We'll have a new contract. With a marriage certificate as an addendum," he stated.

She narrowed her gaze. "Explain."

"I hired you to find a wife to demonstrate to Nestor I've changed. We'll extend our arrangement to you fulfilling the role of the wife. We act like a faithful couple in public, the goal is achieved, and the acquisition goes through."

"And after you get what you want?" His scent wafted over her. It made her think of rumpled bedsheets and hot skin sliding against hers and his mouth…oh, his mouth.

His gaze searched hers. "That's up to us. To you." There was a note in his voice she'd never heard before. It almost sounded tentative.

But Luke didn't do tentative. He cut relationships and walked away. She suspected that was partly why the current situation with Irene got under his skin. He couldn't shun Irene and still work with Nestor.

The late night, the lack of sleep and the churning turmoil in her nervous system made it hard to think. Although even if she had slept a full eight hours it would still be difficult to think when he stood so close. She could see the streaks of dark lapis lazuli in his ocean-blue eyes.

"Danica?"

Too late, she realized he had continued to speak. "I'm sorry?"

"I said this wasn't the way I wanted to ask you. I did want to take you to lunch. Irene forced the timetable."

"I don't—you mean this wasn't just a spur-of-the-moment plan when you saw Irene?" Her heart leapt, just a little.

"I thought of it last night. After you left." His mouth twisted and he reached out to cup her cheek, a brief caress that shouldn't cause her blood to ignite but… "I couldn't sleep."

She shouldn't, in all fairness both to him and to her, agree to marry him. She deserved better than a marriage proposition with all the romance of an annual report presented to the board of directors. He deserved better too, even if he wouldn't admit it.

She had sworn off being involved with men who cared more about their reputation than they did about her. She had been already hurt, badly, by a boyfriend who used people as a stepping stone to getting what he wanted. She swore to never again let her heart be used in that manner.

But her bed was a different matter, as the liquid heat gathering deep in her belly reminded her. As long as she remembered this was a business deal, why not continue to have the best sex imaginable? She nodded, licking her very dry lips. "Yes," she said, her voice rough.

"Yes?" His gaze traced the contours of her mouth.

"Yes," she repeated, but held up her hand when he stepped closer. "Until Ruby Hawk is acquired by the Stavros Group."

His blue eyes darkened, but otherwise he showed no reaction. Was he elated? Deflated? She wished she knew. Finally, a corner of his mouth dented his cheek. "Until the acquisition goes through."

"Deal." She held out her hand to be shaken. He drew her into his arms instead, enveloping her with his strength and warmth. She fought the urge to place her head on his chest, close her eyes and breathe in his scent.

Don't get attached, she sternly warned herself.

"The clock starts now," he rumbled. Right before

his mouth met hers, he whispered, "I'm going to make the time count."

Her last thought, before all ability to form coherent sentences melted away, was her warning came too late.

Eight

In a perfect world, Danica would be thrilled. It was her wedding day. Her groom was a shining star who stood out even in Silicon Valley's crowded galaxy. Her family wouldn't have a financial worry for the foreseeable future. Matt's therapy could continue until he didn't need it, not end when an insurance company cut off the funds. She should be the happiest person walking through the metal detectors at the entrance to the San Mateo County courthouse at that moment.

She was petrified.

In less than twenty-four hours, Luke somehow managed to get a marriage license and arrange for a courthouse ceremony, to be held at two thirty in the afternoon on the dot. The only thing she oversaw was showing up. Which she managed to do, barely, after an hours-long wrestling match with her conscience in the wee hours of the night and a long talk with her roommate, Mai, in the morning.

She inhaled, counted to three, then exhaled. This was strictly business. They had a contract, drawn up after he left her office yesterday. She was walking into this marriage with her eyes open.

She had only herself to blame if she went into it with her emotions wide open too.

"Danica!" Luke was already in the waiting area, early. His crisp azure blue shirt matched his eyes, and his charcoal suit fit him as if it had been made for him, as it no doubt had been. Judging by the looks thrown their way by the others nearby, she was considered to be a lucky bride indeed.

If only they knew.

"Hey. You're here." She managed to sound normal. Inside, she was shaking so hard, she was surprised she could keep her eyes focused.

"You look…" His voice trailed off. "You wore your hair down." He tucked a curl behind her ear, her skin burning where he brushed it. "You're beautiful."

A white lacy gown would have been absurd under the circumstances, but when she saw the pink floral shift dress hanging in the window of a Palo Alto boutique, she went ahead and splurged. "Thanks," she said, suddenly shy from all the eyes on them. She turned her head, so his kiss landed on her cheek. "I don't see Aisha. Let me call her."

"I'm here!" a woman's voice sang out. Danica turned and saw her investigator making her way to them. They needed one witness for the marriage certificate, and when Mai couldn't rearrange her shift at the hospital on such short notice, Danica called Aisha. She was not only a colleague but a friend and the most trustworthy person Danica knew. Aisha was paid well to keep people's secrets private, and Danica was sure she would be discreet about the wedding, as well.

Aisha was stunning in her full-skirted dress, her dark skin glowing against the daffodil yellow fabric. She gave Danica a once-over with her shrewd gaze, then handed a small bouquet of white roses to her. "Brought these just in case. Looks like you might need them."

"I knew there was something I forgot." Danica's smile was only half-faked. "You look great."

"Not every day I get to be a bridesmaid at the last minute," Aisha laughed. "How did you arrange this so fast anyway?"

"Friend-of-the-family favor." Luke said. His phone buzzed, and he looked at the screen. "If you two will excuse me? I'll be right back."

Danica watched him leave. When Aisha touched her shoulder, she jumped.

"That's some bridal nerves," Aisha deadpanned.

"Yeah, well, y'know." Danica's gaze focused on Luke's receding back.

"Actually, I don't. Can we talk privately? Before the groom returns?"

Danica wrenched her gaze away. Aisha sounded serious. And when she was serious, it meant whatever she had to say wasn't good news. "What's up?"

"Cinco Jackson. Why is he calling my office and asking about you? Does it have something to do with this sudden wedding?"

"He's asking about me? What did he say?" Danica's nerves were already scrambled. This put them into a blender set on high.

Aisha shrugged. "How long have I worked with you, did I know you well, how long you have worked for Dallas, general stuff like that."

Danica searched Aisha's gaze. "Did you tell him about the wedding?" Luke planned to put out an announcement eventually, but without mentioning the date. Just a general "Luke Dallas and Danica Novak are pleased to announce their marriage. The bride and groom will reside in Atherton, etc."

"Of course not!" Aisha scoffed. "That's your personal business. But a few days ago, you had me checking on women's marital statuses, and now you're the one getting married? Jackson isn't the only one who is curious."

She sounded miffed. Danica didn't have many friends in California. She didn't want to lose this one. "It's…a spur-of-the-moment decision. But one we've thought through."

"Right." Aisha didn't look convinced, and why would she? Danica's words didn't make sense to herself. "Dallas is incredibly well connected, his mother practically owns Bay Area society, and yet it's just the two of you plus me here for the ceremony?"

Danica tried again. "We didn't want a circus. Just us."

Aisha's expression was still skeptical. "Word on the

street is there's some sort of snag with the Ruby Hawk acquisition, and that snag is the Stavros family and whatever they have on Dallas. I don't know what's going on, but I've done some work for Irene and you do not want to be on her bad side."

"Why would marrying Luke put me on Irene's bad side?" Danica widened her gaze.

Aisha regarded her for a beat. "Hey, if that's the way you want to play it, fine with me. Like I said, it's your life."

"There's nothing—"

Luke walked back to them. He offered his arm to Danica, causing the hyperactive butterflies in her stomach to go into overdrive. "Shall we?" he said. "We're up."

From what she was told later by Aisha, it was a perfectly adequate ceremony. She remembered nothing except squeaking out her responses at the appropriate time and the warm pressure, over far too soon, of Luke's lips on hers. The rest was a blur. Before she knew it, they stood outside the courthouse, the crushed bouquet still in Danica's hands.

"Congratulations, again," Aisha said. "I have to get back to work, but you two go celebrate." She hugged Danica tightly. "I was wrong," she whispered into Danica's ear. "He stares at you like you're a rare steak and he's a contestant on a wilderness-survival show who hasn't eaten in a week." She drew back and gave Danica a wide smile. "Call me. But I expect you to be otherwise occupied for a month, maybe two." She waggled her eyebrows as punctuation.

Danica laughed, even though Aisha was wrong. If Luke looked at her with any hunger, it was because he wanted the acquisition and she was the means to achieving it. Aisha waved goodbye and then Danica was alone.

With Luke. Her husband. Her mouth suddenly was parched and the world spun, once, before it righted itself.

He cleared his throat. "I still owe you that lunch. Hungry?"

Since she had barely been able to eat a bite since he'd walked into her office the day before, she nodded.

"Good." He took her hand. The left one, now sporting a three-carat diamond. "Your fingers are cold."

His weren't. "I did just get married. Better cold fingers than cold feet, I suppose." She tried to smile at him. She was somewhat successful.

His grip tightened. "Thank you, again."

"A deal is a deal. And it's only until you secure the acquisition."

A crease appeared between his eyebrows. "But in the meantime, we are married."

"Of course," she said lightly. "We are. But it's not like that was a real ceremony." She was babbling, but she couldn't stop it.

"I have a certificate that says otherwise."

."I know. But—" she threw out her free hand "—my family wasn't there. And no organist playing 'My Shot' from *Hamilton*."

He stopped walking, causing her to jerk to a stop. "*What* is the organist playing?"

"I can't have 'Here Comes the Bride' played at my wedding. I hate everything about it."

He laughed. It made him devastatingly handsome, his eyes crinkling in the corners. "Of course. Who doesn't?"

"It's such a cliché." She could feel herself relaxing, her shoulders descending to their normal position as they resumed walking. "It's practically a parody of itself. Give me something with more personal meaning."

"And the song you mentioned?"

"It's about taking all the opportunities life hands you. Taking a risk. Like—" She stopped, suddenly aware of who she was talking to. And why.

"Like marriage." He nodded. "I get it." They reached his car and he unlocked the passenger door and ushered her in.

"Like love," she added under her breath while he went around to the driver's side and slid behind the steering wheel. The car didn't have the largest interior to begin with. With him in it, all the oxygen seemed to suddenly disappear. All she had to do was move her hand and she could stroke his thigh. "Where are you taking me to lunch?" She winced. It had come out far too loud.

"That's up to you." He pushed the ignition button and the car purred to life. "I know a nice place not too far from here. Or…"

"Or?"

He turned to her. With a shiver, she realized perhaps Aisha wasn't too off base in her estimation. He did look hungry. The tiger was back. "Or," he said in a deep rumble, picking up her hand and pressing a kiss in her palm, "we go to my place."

Heat instantly pooled between her legs. "You weren't kidding about this being a real marriage."

He shook his head, his blue gaze watching her closely. "No. But as I said, up to you." His thumb gently caressed the back of her hand, drawing lazy circles. Her breasts ached to have the same attention paid to them.

He was hers now. Well, legally, and for as long as the contract was in effect. This may be a business arrangement, but she'd agreed because of the perks that went with it. Like a naked Luke Dallas, tangled in sweaty sheets, about to ensure his prowess would leave her unable to see straight. She smiled and let her hand settle on his thigh. "Do you have champagne at home?"

His blue gaze turned indigo dark. "On ice."

She leaned her torso toward him until their mouths almost touched. "I'm in the mood. For champagne," she whispered against his lips.

He raised his hands and tangled them in her hair. "So am I. But not for champagne." Then he kissed her, insistent, demanding, thoroughly ravaging her mouth until stars pinwheeled around her. She whimpered, irrationally angry at the center console that separated their seats, and he broke away, his breathing heavy. He put the car into drive and they sped out of the parking lot.

This—the way she instantly flared into flame at his touch, the taunt excitement that tortured and pleased them both—would be enough. She could make it be enough. She wouldn't have love, but she would have passion. She could be happy with that, for the duration of their time together.

Or so she told herself.

Danica put down the phone, happy to finish her conversation with her parents and Matt. Then she felt guilty for being happy. True to his word, Luke had paid Danica her promised fee plus bonus the day after the wedding, and she'd sent it to her family. Knowing she secured their house for the time being had been almost enough to make up for the twinges of conscience that had come with announcing her marriage to Luke. Her parents had been shocked she'd wed a man they hadn't met, and she'd finally gotten out of that discussion by promising she and Luke would visit them as soon as Matt, whose recovery still moved too slowly, felt up to it. The weekly conversations since had been still a bit awkward, but so far she'd managed to answer their questions to their satisfaction.

She opened a file on her computer. Since the wedding, life had settled into something resembling a routine, if *routine* could ever be a word applied to life with Luke Dallas. Luke still needed a director to run Ruby Hawk's community outreach, and Danica had several new candidates to interview. She also had to finish a report on the charitable causes the foundation could support, as Luke wanted Ruby Hawk's technology to be involved.

What she should be doing, however, was concentrating on her business plan for her own executive-search company. She wouldn't be at Ruby Hawk forever.

But facing up to that reality meant facing up to her inevitable parting from Luke. When she'd agreed to marry Luke, she'd known sex with him could be mind-blowing fun. She'd had no idea their first night only scratched the surface of the erotic gratification in store.

When work hours were over and they were alone... she shivered, her mind filled with images from the night before. His mouth, hot, plundering, exploring every inch of her skin, his tongue taking her to heights she didn't know existed before she shattered into mind-less shards. She never imagined—

As if her thoughts conjured him up, he walked into her office, his head down as he read something on his smartphone. Her heart gave a skip and a hop, noting the way his tailored shirt hugged his chest, skimmed over the six-pack of abs she knew was underneath. It would be the work of only a few buttons and her hands could glide over his skin...

He stopped in front of her desk. "Did you put to-gether this proposal for using Ruby Hawk's technol-ogy to make youth sports leagues safer?" he asked.

Ah. He was in work mode. She'd have to save those thoughts until that night. "Is there something wrong?"

"Not at all. It's good." He put the phone in his pocket and sat on the edge of her desk. "Why didn't you say you were passionate about injuries in youth sports? Did you play?"

"Me?" She laughed. "I'm the proverbial wrong-way kid. My first soccer game, I kicked two goals for the other team. I'm much better at providing moral sup-port."

"But you must have some knowledge. This is a very persuasive proposal. You obviously care deeply about the subject."

She wasn't sure if she wanted Luke to probe into her personal life. They were married but their intimacy was strictly physical. The one area she could keep separate from him was her family. If she let him in, all the way, she might not have the strength to walk away when their contract ended. She chewed on her lower lip.

"I've done a lot of reading about concussions and their effect on the brain. Don't get me wrong—involvement in team sports is beneficial. But Ruby Tech has an opportunity to put sensors using its biofeedback algorithms into equipment to make it safer."

He nodded. "The proposal is very clear on those points. You should talk to one of the lead engineers, however. It's hazy when it comes to tech specs."

"See?" She smiled. "I knew there was something wrong with it."

He got up from her desk and started for the door, allowing her to admire his perfect rear end in action. But instead of exiting he turned around to face her. "This is a good proposal. Stop selling yourself short."

A tendril of exasperation curled up her spine. "I don't."

"You do. You could be the foundation director if you wanted."

"I like recruitment."

"You could do more."

This felt like caring, coming from him. But it wasn't. She was merely a convenient means to an end. That

the sex curled all their toes was just the cherry on this
sundae. She had to keep reminding herself. "I'm good
at what I do."

"I didn't say you weren't. I said you could do more.
Make a difference."

"Search does make a difference. I find people good
jobs."

"I'm giving you a compliment."

"And I said thank you."

"I—" His phone rang, much to Danica's relief. She
watched him take it out of his pocket and answer it.
Then she watched a shutter fall over his expression,
turning it blank and emotionless. "Yes… No… Yes…"
he said at different intervals. Then he hung up and
turned to leave her office. His movements were rigid,
his shoulders held tight.

Her anger was doused, replaced by concern. She
got up from her chair and blocked him from exiting.
"Who was on the phone?"

"No one," he said. "I'll see you at home tonight."

She narrowed her gaze. "What's wrong? Cinco Jackson? Nestor? Irene?" The last name tasted like vinegar
on her lips.

Irene had been friendly—too friendly. Every day
brought a new invitation: lunch, a shopping trip, tick-
ets to a charity event, seats at the San Francisco Symphony. Danica finally attended a tea to benefit a local
women's shelter. Much to her surprise, Danica enjoyed
herself. Irene was friendly and very charming. No wonder Luke had had an off-and-on "benefits" relationship with her.

He shook his head as if trying to shoo off a winged insect. "An appointment I thought would be cancelled."

The phone screen in his hand was flashing. "You're getting another phone call."

He cursed under his breath. Then he answered. "What? I just hung up with her... I said I would be there... No... I said, no." His index finger punched End, but not before Danica saw the caller ID. Jonathan Dallas.

"Family?" she asked.

"My father," he agreed.

"That's the appointment?" She knew Luke's father had retired to West Palm Beach, Florida, while his mother and her current husband traveled between their homes in San Francisco, Paris and Cape Town. "Is he in town? Should we invite him over for dinner?"

His mouth twisted. "Hell, no. Lunch on neutral ground is bad enough. They're suggesting we meet in Half Moon Bay. Driving over the mountains in the middle of a work day is supposed to be convenient for me."

His phone rang again. This time the caller ID read Phoebe Ailes. Luke hit a button and the ringing stopped. He put the phone in his pocket and regarded Danica. "You should consider taking the foundation job."

Nice try. She wasn't biting. "If your parents are in town, why haven't I met them?"

"You're being nosy." It was not a compliment.

"I'm always nosy. It's what I do. I pry into people's lives so I can find the right employment fit."

"I have a job. To which I need to get back." His words were reinforced with steel.

She sighed and stepped aside. "Fine. But if you want to talk about your family, I'm here."

"I wouldn't wish that on anyone. Especially not on you." He opened the door.

Danica was no stranger to Luke's moods. He could be cold, dictatorial even, when people tried to cross him. But when the discussions were reasonable or philosophical, he was thoughtful, witty even. In their bed, he could be tender—so tender it caused her heart to ache with a longing she didn't dare dwell on.

Right now he looked bruised. She never thought Luke could be hurt by others, much less his own parents. She couldn't imagine not cherishing family and being cherished by them in return. The realization punctured her heart.

"I want to go to lunch with you."

He blinked. She felt a momentary burst of pride. It took a lot to surprise him.

"No, you don't." His tone was final.

"Yes, I do." No, she didn't. She was scared spitless. And it meant canceling her appointment to look at a promising commercial real-estate site for her agency. But his parents were another piece to the puzzle that was Luke.

"Are you sure? The reason for the lunch is they heard about the marriage." He grimaced. "Not from me."

"You didn't—" Her mouth snapped shut and she

took three deep breaths. "Why wouldn't you tell them about me? It's not like it's a real marriage."

"It's not that. I didn't tell them because..." He shrugged. "Because in the bigger scheme, they didn't need to know."

She silently counted to ten. "Of course, they need to know if you're married! You're their son."

"The only concerns my parents have about my marriage are how much value you bring to the family coffers and/or how much it will take to buy you off when necessary. I was hoping to avoid the confrontation."

Now it was her turn to blink. "You're kidding."

"No. You sure you want to come to lunch?" He obviously expected her to say no.

He forgot she was the one who bet all her money on a turn of the roulette wheel. "I need to meet them at some point. After all, we're married, even if there is an expiration date."

"It's your funeral."

"Oh, come on." She smoothed faint wrinkles from the shoulders of his shirt. "It can't be that bad."

It was, exactly, that bad. Danica and Luke arrived at the upscale bistro at one o'clock on the dot, thanks to Luke's sports car. She gripped the armrest the entire way as he sped along the twisty mountain roads he took to avoid the traffic on the freeways. She was still recovering from the last switchback he took while overtaking another vehicle.

"Feeling better?" Luke asked.

"Save your concern for the driver of the minivan

we passed. I think you took ten years off that man's life." She smoothed back escaped tendrils of hair. They bounced back to framing her face as soon as her hand fell to her side. Luke reached out and twisted a curl around his finger.

"I prefer it down." The rumble of his voice and the stroke of his thumb on her cheek nearly took her knees out. Luckily for her, the hostess returned with a wide smile on her face.

"I'll take you to the rest of your party." The hostess beckoned, and Luke reached out for Danica's hand without looking at her. The automatic gesture caused her to smile. She was still smiling when they arrived at the secluded patio table set for four. Two of the chairs were occupied, but the occupants were busy staring at their phones.

Luke cleared his throat. His grip on her hand tightened.

The older man, who had to be Luke's father, looked up. "Well, hello there! Glad to see both of you," he said with a cheery smile. "I'm Jonathan."

"This is—" Luke began.

"We know who she is," the older woman said, still staring at her phone. "Just not from you." Luke's mother was blonde and fair skinned, but Danica couldn't discern any other distinguishing features thanks to the oversize sunglasses dominating her face.

"This is Danica," Luke finished. "Danica, my parents. Jonathan Dallas and Phoebe Ailes." He tightened his grip on her hand. "Don't say I didn't warn you," he breathed into her ear.

Danica nudged him sharply with her elbow and then removed her hand to hold it out to his mother. "Pleased to meet you, Mrs. Ailes."

Luke's mother looked up from her phone screen at the proffered hand, gave it one firm pump and let it go in favor of returning to her device. "Likewise," she said, not a flicker of emotion on her expression. Her sunglasses remained on.

Luke pulled out the empty chair next to his father for Danica and helped her into it. "Call her Phoebe," he said. "I do."

His father reached for Danica's hand and carried it to his lips. "Very charmed to meet such a lovely lady," Jonathan said after slowly releasing her fingers.

"Thank you." Danica smiled at Luke's father. He was a remarkably handsome man. But there wasn't much of a resemblance between father and son. Jonathan was Teflon slick, from his carefully coiffed salt-and-pepper hair to his impeccably manicured nails. Nor did Danica see much of Phoebe in Luke. His mother resembled a diamond, all polished and glittering surfaces, from her caramel-streaked hair shining like a helmet in the sun to the heavy gold chains wrapped around her neck and wrists.

Luke consisted of rough edges and dangerous angles. His dark hair was tousled, a sure signal he had run his hands through it more than once, his heavy brows drawn together. That was fine with Danica. She preferred the brooding man of the moors to his magazine-glossy parents.

"So." Phoebe finally put down the phone. "This is

a surprise. Luke said you were too busy to join us. Danielle, is it?"

"Danica." Luke took the seat next to his mother and across from Danica. His loafer-clad foot nudged hers. "You know her name. And she cleared her schedule for this, so be nice."

His mother waved him off. "Perhaps if you had told us you were married, instead of leaving us to find out from Irene Stavros of all people, I would be better acquainted with my new daughter-in-law's name."

Danica shot a look at Luke.

Luke shook his head, once. His loafer nudged her ballet-slipper flats under the table again, and then he cleared his throat. "Few people knew about the wedding. Danica and I decided we wanted something quiet and private."

Luke's mother huffed and launched into a rejoinder, but Danica didn't hear her. Of *course* Irene told Luke's parents. Wasn't the reason Luke needed to find a wife because of the Stavros-Dallas feud? They belonged to the same world of high finance and cutthroat business deals, private jets and unlimited bank accounts. While she...she was just a temporary interloper. With a temporary contract.

"Is something wrong, dear?" Phoebe's eyebrows rose above the rim of her sunglasses.

"Not a thing," Danica said, flipping open her menu and running her gaze down the page. "What is everyone having? I can't decide."

"You're so pale." Phoebe's tone shifted, turning so

sweet it could be used to trap wasps. "You're not…
queasy, I hope? Or faint?"

"No. I'm fine." Aside from the fact that meeting
Phoebe and Jonathan thrust Danica's sham arrangement into the light, exposing shady corners she pur-
posefully tried to avoid.

Luke snapped his menu open. "The ceviche here
is good," he said to Danica. "You'd like it. Raw fish,
no spice."

"Raw fish? I don't think that's advisable," Phoebe
said. "Perhaps the petit filet mignon, although of course
one needs to be careful of listeria."

"Listeria?" Danica raised her eyebrows at Luke. "Is
that like mad cow or E. coli?"

"She's not pregnant, Phoebe." Luke turned to Danica. "Listeria is a food-based bacterium that can cause
serious health issues during pregnancy. Care to split
the ceviche as an appetizer?"

"How do you know that?" Danica asked Luke.

"Ordering meals with Anjuli when she was pregnant
with her twins," Luke answered. "Maybe you should
get your own ceviche. I know how much you like your
fish."

Phoebe cleared her throat. Danica and Luke turned
to look at her. "If she's not pregnant, then why did you
rush into marriage?" She took her sunglasses off, revealing piercing dark blue eyes. They seemed to be
the only feature her son inherited. But while Luke's
gaze could be cold and distant, it was never as icy as
the arctic blast directed at Danica.

"Define 'rush,'" Luke answered. "How do you feel

about lobster rolls as a main course?" he asked Danica. "This place is famous for them."

"Wait—you think I'm pregnant?" Danica blinked several times in Phoebe's direction, struggling to wrap her mind around the question. Sure, she and Luke frequently engaged in the activity required for creating a child, but even if she were pregnant—and she wasn't—she would barely be aware of it herself. A chuckle escaped her lips as she turned to face Luke. "Is this a question every woman you bring to meet your parents receives, or just me?"

Phoebe closed her menu and put it down on the plate in front of her, careful to square the corners so they were aligned perfectly with the plane of the table. "My son has never been married before, Danielle. And certainly not to someone whom we've never met, whose name barely shows up in a web search, much less on any social rosters of any import."

"You've learned to use a web browser. Good for you," Luke said. "Let's cut to the chase. You wanted to inspect my wife. Here she is. She even agreed to the inspection, which says far more about her than any internet search could. Now, can we order?"

Jonathan cleared his throat. "It's a rare occasion when I can have lunch with my son and his beautiful wife." He patted Danica's hand where it rested on the table's surface. "It's such a nice day, wouldn't you agree? I do miss living here at times. Tell me, did you grow up in California?"

"No, Rhode Island."

"Ah, Newport! I know it quite well. Do you sail?

I've always said there is nothing in a man's soul that can't be cured by an hour of wind in your hair and sea salt in your face. Bracing!" He chuckled, his eyes crinkling in the corners.

"Sorry, I don't sail," Danica said. "And you probably know Newport better than I do."

"Tennis, then. Surely you play. We must have you out to the club when you come to Florida. Doubles, perhaps, although you two kids would wipe us old folks off the court. Speaking of—" he turned to Luke "—your stepmother and I are at the top of doubles ladder this month, again. The interclub tournament should be a cakewalk this year. At the board meeting, I told them the club is going to need a bigger trophy case. Ha!" He guffawed. "The guys at the club are still laughing."

"Danica isn't much for organized sports," Luke said, flashing a conspiratorial grin in her direction.

"No?" Jonathan's eyebrows met in the middle of his forehead. "Golf?"

She shook her head.

"What about skiing? That's not too organized. Especially not the way we do it." He chuckled and shook his head. "By the time we arrive in Vail and open the house, it's too late to hit the slopes. We hit the schnapps."

"Sure. I ski," Danica said. She had a feeling if she didn't land on a sport, Jonathan would continue to quiz her until he found one. And it wasn't a lie. Much. In high school she went on a school trip to a ski resort in New Hampshire and fell down the bunny slope a few times.

"Great!" Jonathan flashed two rows of very white, very straight teeth at her. "It's settled. Christmas in Colorado."

"Dad—" Luke began.

"Oh, please, Jonathan." Phoebe cut off her son. "One, you just met the girl. Two, no one knows who she is or what she wants from Luke. This…whatever it is…came wholly out of the blue and I can't believe you're swallowing this malarkey. Three, you have no idea if she will still be around next week, much less by Christmas. Four, Irene said—"

"All right." The thunderclouds building on Luke's expression erupted into a storm. He stood up. "You wanted a meeting, you got one. It's now over." He put his hands on the back of Danica's chair, ready to pull it out so she could stand up. "Danica, let's go."

"Lucas Dallas, sit down," Phoebe commanded. "We're not done, and we won't be until we've figured out how to handle this situation you got yourself into. You have very specific obligations to uphold and we need a plan."

"I have a plan," he responded. His gaze caught Danica's. It brimmed with many things, chief among them long-held pain mixed with frustrated exasperation.

And apology. To her. For exposing her to this. Concern, for any discomfort his parents caused her. Her heart squeezed so hard, she was surprised she could still breathe.

He broke contact to look at his parents. "And the plan is we're leaving. Ready?" He offered his hand to Danica.

No. She wasn't ready. She didn't know what to do. What to say. Phoebe wasn't wrong. Danica might still be around for the coming Christmas, but she wouldn't be present for Christmases further in the future. Her relationship with Luke was indeed, from a certain point of view, malarkey.

But not for the reasons Phoebe inferred. Danica didn't want anything from Luke or his family. Certainly not money—although, her guilty conscience piped up, she accepted the consulting gig because of the dollars he promised her. *But it wasn't the reason why you agreed to the marriage*, her libido shot back.

Her heart remained silent, but only because she knew what it would say. She was in love with Luke. Had been, ever since their dinner at the taqueria.

It was also hopeless.

She rose to her feet, wincing at the loud noise as the metal chair scraped across the tiled patio floor. "Mrs. Ailes, I understand your concern. This is the first time you've met me, and I'm married to your son. I would be suspicious if I were in your shoes too."

Luke's gaze flashed a warning signal she would be stupid to ignore.

She did so anyway. "I'll tell you the truth. Your son—"

"Danica." Luke's tone could have carved granite. He wasn't cautioning her to stop speaking. He was demanding.

"Your son," she started again, despite the typhoon of disapproval aimed in her direction, "is a very special man. I didn't want to fall in love with him. I fought it."

Did I ever. "But the more time I spent in his presence, the more it was inevitable."

She didn't dare look at Luke. Still, she sensed he held himself ramrod straight, not moving a muscle. "I know this marriage is sudden, but the emotion is real." *On my side, at least.*

She took a deep breath, and then slowly let it out. "I can't impress you. But you should be very impressed by your son. He deserves your trust and support, in all matters. Including who he marries." *Whoever she will be, after I'm long gone.*

Phoebe stared at Danica throughout her speech, her dark blue gaze unblinking. But at the end, she raised one perfectly groomed eyebrow and nodded, ever so slightly.

"That was a beautiful speech, my dear," Jonathan said. "Just beautiful." He turned to his ex-wife. "See, Phoebe, it won't be a problem getting her to sign a post-nup even though the wedding already occurred. You always did worry over trivial things." He clapped his hands together. "Well, now that we have that settled, let's have a meal. Sit back down, you two."

Danica barely heard him over the whooshing of her pulse beating loudly in her ears. She didn't dare look at Luke. "I need to visit the ladies' room. You three talk." She walked-ran toward the dim, cool interior of the restaurant.

But once she was inside, shivering in the air conditioning, she did not turn down the hallway the hostess indicated to her. Instead she turned right, through the central dining room toward the main exit to the street, and kept walking.

She would never get used to Luke's world. Could never adjust. Ski chalets in Vail, country clubs, social rosters...she shook her head. It was as if she had spent the last half hour in another country. Scotland, maybe. Or Australia. Somewhere where she understood the basic words, but the context was wholly new.

She took in her surroundings for the first time. The main street was lined with restaurants and shops, the kind that had hand-painted wooden signs on the outside but scarves that cost as much as a monthly payment on her student loans displayed inside. A block away she spotted a turquoise bench, flanked by terracotta pots bursting with red geraniums. It was a bit too cheerful for her present mood, but at least she could sit and contemplate her next move.

The bench was warm from the sun, but an ocean breeze kept the temperature pleasant. Good, because her cheeks were hot enough to be a fire hazard. She cringed at the thought of seeing Luke after she'd declared her love for him to his parents, of all people. What must he be thinking? She drew her knees up, encircling them with her arms, and buried her face on top of them.

"You have a habit of running out of restaurants." Luke's solid presence sat down next to her.

She took a deep breath and raised her head. There was a faint smile on his face. He didn't seem upset she had run out on him and his family. If anything, he was a bit wary. As if he didn't know what to expect from her.

And why would he know what to expect, when that speech had surprised herself? Better to get this conversation over with so they can both pretend it never happened and go back to their previous arrangement. She unfolded her limbs and gave him a lopsided smile. "I didn't run out of the taqueria. I even offered to pay."

"I'm also counting the sushi at the benefit."

"Hey, Chef Nagao was the one who ran out. Of fish."

He smiled, but it didn't reach his eyes. His gaze remained wary. "I'm sorry," he said simply.

He was sorry? For what? She was the one who'd opened mouth, inserted foot, ankle and calf. "You have no need to apologize."

He snorted. "You were already doing me a favor by coming to lunch. You didn't have to give that speech too. Now I really owe you."

"A favor?" She unfolded her legs and sat up straight, turning so she could meet his gaze head on. He thought of what she said as a favor? She didn't know whether to be happy at the out he gave her or upset he thought her words weren't 100 percent real. "I didn't—"

He made an impatient sound deep in his throat. "You know what I mean. But that went above and beyond." He picked up her hand, rubbing his thumb across her knuckles. As always, hot lightning sparked where their hands connected and spread through her veins. "I appreciate it, Danica. I appreciate you."

Appreciate. It was a nice word. In the past, she'd

wished Johanna had used it more frequently when applied to her work. But coming from Luke—

It was like being handed a brussels sprout when one craved a steak. She didn't want his appreciation. She wanted his love.

But it wasn't on the menu. She pulled her hand from his and gave him a wide smile. "Just trying to do my temporary husband a solid," she said brightly. "I'm sorry I ran out."

He gave her a one-sided smile. "I'm sorry I put you through that."

His approval wrapped around her like a warm blanket. It should be enough. He gave it so rarely.

But while she enjoyed his appreciation, it wasn't enough. Would never be enough. "You did warn me," she said, plastering a smile on her face. "We should go back to the restaurant, so I can apologize to your parents for being gone so long."

"You mean so they can apologize to you. Which they will. But they left right after you. Seems an earlier tee time for my father just happened to open up, while my mother conveniently forgot she had plans to meet friends in the city." He stood and offered her his right hand. "I know a great burger joint between here and Palo Alto. Interested?"

She nodded and took his hand, his fingers curling around hers, and he pulled her off the bench. It felt so natural to continue to hold his hand as they strolled through the charming downtown on the way back to his car. She paused to point out the terrible wine puns on display in a cheese shop. "Everything happens for a Riesling," she groaned.

"I just called to say Merlot," Luke countered. "Que Syrah, Syrah."

She laughed, turning to resume their journey toward the carpark. But she stopped, just for a second, when she caught a glimpse of their reflection in the shop's window.

They looked like a couple. A real couple. Out for a stroll, enjoying the beautiful weather. Enjoying each other.

But she knew the truth. Luke was engaged in a game of wits with Irene and Nestor Stavros, and she was just a chess piece. She kept her gaze focused on the sidewalk all the way back to the car.

Nine

Luke drove the borrowed truck as fast as the speed limit would allow to Danica's rented house. In the weeks since the marriage, Danica had spent nearly every night at his place, but she still maintained her own place. Finally, he'd put his foot down. It was important this marriage had all the appearances of a real one when Nestor returned to town. She needed to be in full residence at his place, not ping-ponging between two addresses. It surprised him how much he looked forward to seeing her clothes in his closet. Her books on his bookcase. He liked knowing there would be physical proof she was ensconced in his life.

He certainly didn't mind having Danica there at the end of every day. He'd never lived with anyone before—it had never made practical sense—but the longer he spent with Danica, the more the situation appealed to him. Already he could sense his house, purchased for its investment value, becoming a home. A place where he wanted to be, rather than a building in which to store items and sleep. Things were falling into place, neatly and orderly.

Except one. He couldn't tell if Danica wanted to move in as much as he wanted her to. The fisted knot in his stomach tightened. After the lunch with his parents, she had been quiet. Too quiet. He knew it had been a bad idea. But he'd calculated the risk and took it anyway. He'd figured the odds were in his favor, because she had a way of making even the most onerous obligations seem achievable and fun.

Then his parents had had to behave like, well, his parents. As long as he lived, he would always be grateful—and knocked off his feet—that Danica had stood up to them. No, strike that. She'd stood up for *him*. She'd gone toe to toe with the Demon Czarina of Bay Area society and the passive-aggressive charm offensive that was his father—and won.

Luke fought his own battles. He had ever since he could remember. He enjoyed it. He relished the strategy, the countermeasures, the surprise attacks. He thought fifteen steps ahead and eighteen months into the future. By the time his opponents gathered to attack, he had moved onto the next battlefield.

It was unsettling to have a champion. Unsettling, but triggering an almost painful warmth that swelled inside his chest.

He pulled the truck in front of a small, nondescript

house. A chain link fence surrounded a patchy yard, littered with children's toys. Danica ran down the front path to meet him. Raising an eyebrow, he indicated the plastic dump trucks and naked baby dolls. "Something I don't know?"

"My roommate occasionally babysits to make extra money," she said, after accepting a kiss. "She has a good job as a pediatric nurse, but costs have skyrocketed the last few years." The front door opened directly into the living room, and she ushered Luke inside. The late afternoon sunshine barely pierced through the curtains lining the windows and did little to dispel the shadows. Still, he could see the room was well kept, even if most of the furniture had seen better days. Several cardboard boxes were stacked neatly against a wall.

"You didn't tell me you shared a house," he said.

"When I moved here, I didn't realize how expensive it is to live in the Bay Area. I was lucky Mai needed someone to rent her spare room and we hit it off. It worked out well. So, um…" Danica played with the bracelet on her wrist. "Thanks for coming over. But I was happy to call movers."

She was being tentative. Just like she'd been after the lunch with his parents. "Glad to help. Besides, I keep missing my trainer appointments. Someone, not naming names, keeps me occupied in bed in the early morning."

She laughed, and he relaxed. Maybe it was just nerves. They were legally married, but living together was a big step.

It didn't take long to load Danica's possessions from the front room. Mai owned most of the furniture, so it remained with the house. He frowned after they placed the last box inside the truck.

"What about the bedroom?" he asked. The ever-present spark when he was near Danica ignited even though now was not the time. No doubt the bed was stripped of its sheets and pillows. Too bad, because he couldn't think of a better way to recuperate from a short afternoon of moving medium-size boxes than by snuggling under the covers. And by *snuggling*, he meant hearing her breathily scream his name at least two or three times before burying himself in her warm depth.

"Um." Danica suddenly couldn't meet his gaze. "Everything I'm taking is in these boxes."

"In case you've forgotten, you're moving in with me today."

"What do you think you loaded into the truck?"

"A partial load."

Her eyes darkened. "We agreed I would live with you as your wife. I'm doing that. The sooner we get to your place, the sooner I can unpack."

Logically, she was right. He didn't care. It smacked of the false reassurances his parents would give him whenever a stepparent moved in or out. *Oh, they're just moving some unwanted things elsewhere, don't worry.* Or, *You can leave a few toys here, but maybe take the rest to your mom's house. What do you say? Just for now.* It was never "just for now." It was always forever.

"Where's your bedroom?"

"Down the left hallway. Why?"

He picked up an empty box and strode off.

"Oh, no, you don't." Danica caught up to him just as he reached what had to be her room. Here the heavy curtains were tied back to let in golden sunshine that accentuated the cheerful profusion of bright colors and floral prints. Artwork decorated the walls, and photos were crowded next to books on the shelves.

He thrust the box at her. "Get packing."

She rolled her eyes. "Stop being ridiculous. I'm keeping some of my things here, that's all."

"Why?"

Her gaze wouldn't meet his. "I honestly didn't think you would mind."

He did. More than he thought possible. "Not answering my question. Why—"

Then realization dropped on his head like an anvil. "Do you think I will throw you out of my house when the contract is over?"

Red flooded her averted cheek.

It matched the shade filling his vision. "How could you—you don't trust me?"

Her gaze continued to fix on a point far to his right. "It's not that. But—"

"But you don't." The ground shifted under his feet, throwing everything he thought was solid and sure into question.

She sighed. "Our agreement is only until the Ruby Hawk deal is signed. That's less than a month away. So I asked Mai if I could continue to rent the room."

"I've been honest with you at every step—"

"Yes, but the steps keep changing! I was supposed to find you a bride. Not be the bride. Who knows what your next strategy will be?"

The room turned dark and muddled, the color running together in a muddy mess. "I wasn't aware you disliked being married to me," he managed to say.

Her eyes widened. "No! That's not what I mean! I love—" She stopped, and then pressed her lips together. "I am more than happy with our arrangement. But it has an end date. You don't expect me to hang around after it is over." She met his gaze straight on. "Do you?"

Did he?

He hadn't thought much past the completion of the deal with Nestor. By now, he should have gathered up all the data points and run a regression analysis to determine the natural course forward. But he had no plans past signing the paperwork with Nestor.

He and Danica could make a plan. Together.

He opened his mouth but was cut off by a shake of her head. "No, of course you don't. And I didn't expect you to."

Her dismissal stung. Like an entire colony of fire ants. "You won't be tossed aside." He used his CEO voice. "That would be a waste of invested time and resources."

She flinched, just a millimeter, before she recovered with a smirk that didn't reach her eyes. "Spoken like someone who values heartlessness."

That stung even more. "A heartless person would walk away. Not my intention."

"A heartless person is someone who views others as objects only. No emotion. No love," she finished in a rush. "Let's get the boxes over to your house. Then Operation Living Together can commence." She moved to walk toward the front room.

She would not distract him by changing the subject. "You say I'm heartless. So be it. But you're refusing to trust. That's worse."

She whirled around, her hands thrown into the air. "How can I trust you when there's no emotion?"

"It didn't seem to get in your way last night. And this morning." She trusted him enough to shatter in his arms, crying his name as he shuddered inside her.

She flushed. "Yes, the sex is great. I admit it. But sex is a, what did you call it? 'Chemical reaction caused by hormones and preprogrammed neurological responses'?" She quoted his words from the taqueria back at him. "When there's no lo—caring," she corrected herself, "there can't be trust."

"People trust each other every day without being emotionally involved," he pointed out with perfect logic. "Trust is what allows society to function. If we didn't trust firemen to show up when called or banks to hold our money—"

"Or Nestor to hold up his end of the deal?" Her direct stare challenged him.

"Yes," he agreed. "Or business deals."

"And there's the rub. I don't trust Nestor or Irene either."

He shook his head. "There's a difference between

blind trust and expecting someone to hold up their end of the deal—"

"Which you can't trust Nestor and Irene to do, because they don't care about you. They want something from you instead."

On the contrary, they *did* care. About winning. About getting the upper hand in the game of one-upmanship their families had played for decades.

He was still furious with Irene for telling his parents about his marriage. That was underhanded, even for her. His parents always looked down on his efforts to be his own man, build his own legacy. It was the twenty-first century, but they held Victorian notions that working for a living would degrade their social position. They would have been the first to urge him to take the offered money and give up his company, even to Nestor, if it meant he would join them in spending the family trust jetting from golf course to ski slope.

Irene knew that. Siccing his parents on him while wrestling control of his company was just an added bonus for her. "That's not precisely true—"

"You know what I think?" Her words tumbled out quickly, as if a dam holding back a swollen river had finally burst. "You don't want to believe in caring—in *love*—because it would mean giving up control. And you can't stand not being in control. You want to corral the entire world, turn it into nice neat equations. But the world doesn't work that way."

What? No. He didn't believe in love because it wasn't real. Oxytocin and other hormones tricked the brain into attachment, and smart humans learned how to manipulate that to get what they wanted. Trust, on the other hand, was a cerebral choice, born of rationality and logic. It was the most powerful covenant possible between two people.

And he trusted her. Not just with the deal, but with his real self. The self who bought his own computer by gambling online while still in middle school. The man who no longer needed his parents' approval but wouldn't mind having it, on his terms.

She'd learn to place her trust in him. They still had time before their prenup came to its conclusion. And he was confident they could make an even more advantageous deal when this agreement came to its end.

The sun outside the windows started its descent, casting a golden glow over the room. It lit her curls, turning them into a halo that framed her heart-shaped face. Hazy rays outlined the curves of her hips and waist, reminding him how well he knew her unique geography but still had more to explore. His gaze dropped to her lips, pursed into an eminently kissable shape. Her cheeks were rosy, her gaze dark and wide.

His groin tightened. He and Danica may disagree on emotion, but when it came to physical activities, they came together. Many times. Each explosion more mind-shattering than the last.

"I thought you liked my control," he said, moving toward her until only inches separated them. He brushed a loose curl off her cheek, allowing his fingers to linger on the soft smoothness of her skin. "A lot," he breathed into her ear.

She blinked. Her crossed arms relaxed, her body

tilting toward his. Several emotions, few of which he could identify, came and went on her face. She settled on a half smile, her closed lips softly curving. "You're trying to change the subject."

"Is it working?" He kissed the skin where her neck met her shoulder, breathing in her delectable scent.

She let out a soft gasp and inclined her head to give him more access. "I didn't tell you the best part about rooming with Mai. She has a double shift today. She won't be home until 10:00 p.m."

He grinned. The knot in his gut loosened, untied. Sex was familiar. Sex, he could handle. "Really?" he rumbled.

She nodded, that mischievous pink tongue of hers appearing as she licked her upper lip. "I have the house to myself," she breathed, and wound her arms around his neck.

"Good to know," he replied. He started to remove the elastic from her ponytail, but she moved away.

"No."

He stared at her. "No?"

She nodded. "My house, my rules. And rule number one—" she stood on tiptoe so she could whisper in his ear, her breath hot against his skin "—is no touching. I get to touch you. Let's see how you can handle not being in control."

Danica focused on Luke, her hands gripping his tightly. When they made love, Luke ensured she was awash in pleasure before he would allow himself to take his. Even moving into his house had to be on his terms, the shots called by him.

After meeting his parents, she had a better idea of what drove Luke. Far better to separate love from sex or remove love from the equation altogether when marriage was a game of power. He'd warned her, but she hadn't believed it. Then she'd seen it with her own eyes.

She couldn't change him. She couldn't make him see winning wasn't the only thing. In fact, it didn't even make the top one hundred of things that make life worth living. She couldn't make him believe unconditional love had a power of its own, so great it could move worlds.

But for now, he was in her hands. Literally. She was the one in charge. "No touching," she reiterated, and stepped back. "If you do, I'll stop."

She dropped his hands just long enough to grab a long piece of fabric from the organizer hanging on the back of her door while his hopeful gaze focused on the queen-size bed that dominated the space in her small bedroom. By the time his attention turned back to her, she had finished looping the item around his wrists and tying them behind his back with a square knot.

He looked over his shoulder, straining to see his hands. "What in the world did you use?"

"Hogwarts school tie from a trip to Universal Studios," she said. "I'm a Hufflepuff."

He shook his head. "I have no idea what that means." Then he wagged his eyebrows. "But I like the sound of huffing and puffing."

"I suppose that makes you the Big Bad Wolf."

He growled, making her laugh. She began to unbutton his shirt, pausing to trail her fingers through the crisp hair outlining his pecs. His flat brown nipples just begged to be touched, and with her thumbs she drew circles, ever so softly, over each one.

A shudder racked his body, and he leaned down to kiss her. She stepped back just in time and wagged a finger in front of his tempting lips. "No touching."

"I thought you meant with my hands."

"Don't think," she breathed in his ear, then nipped his earlobe. "Feel."

His blue eyes were even darker. "Don't worry, that's happening."

"If you're talking, you're thinking," she warned and scraped her nails across his nipples. His Adam's apple worked for a few beats, and the erection she could feel against her stomach pressed harder.

She stepped back, just a smidge, so her right hand could follow the dark trail leading down his muscled stomach and disappearing into his khaki trousers. The front of his pants sported an impressive bulge. It took only a second to undo his belt and then both her hands were free to slip between the waistband of his boxer briefs and the firm skin of his lower abdomen, exploring the straining prize awaiting her.

Luke's breath came in staggered bursts. His hips bucked, brushing against her. When she took her hands away, he stopped.

"Danica." Her name was a strangled combination of syllables.

She grinned. Giving his erection one last caress,

she moved away to slowly unbutton her blouse, pausing after each one to see if he was watching. His gaze was glued to her chest. She let the silk fabric fall to the floor and shimmied out of her skirt. When her relationship with Luke turned physical, Danica had decided she needed to invest in new lingerie. Today's matched set was nude-colored lace trimmed with black satin ribbons. She chose the bra because it created cleavage for days, while the wisp of lace covering her bottom seemingly revealed everything yet left most to the imagination.

She didn't need to be psychic to know where Luke's imagination was leading him. His hungry gaze followed her as she walked back to him. Placing a hand on his chest, proud of herself for controlling the tremble caused by the near-feral expression on his face, she helped him step out of his pants and underwear. Then she carefully steered him backward toward the wing chair in the corner of the room. He sank down into it, his gaze never once leaving hers.

She could get lost in the heat she saw there. The heat and the need and the… No. She would not delude herself there was anything resembling caring in his gaze. He liked sex, and he liked having sex with her. That was all. Still, a tiny corner of her heart began to beat in hopeful rhythm.

Keeping her eyes focused on his, she found his erection, even bigger than before. She resumed her strokes, firm followed by soft and going back to firm again. He stifled a sound deep in his throat as his eyes rolled back, his head falling against the chair. Then she knelt in front of him and replaced her hands with her mouth, her tongue continuing the rhythm.

His loud groan pierced straight to her core. The liquid heat gathering between her legs burst into greedy conflagration. She pressed her legs together to relieve some tension. This was about him, not her. Still, she wasn't sure if she would be the one to break down and ask for completion.

"Danica, I—" his voice was strained "—need to touch you."

She redoubled her efforts, lost in his scent and his taste and the sheer pleasure of having him at her mercy. He was close. She could feel it.

"Danica," he growled. "Please. Please."

Please? The word was so unexpected, she lost her rhythm and fell backward on her heels. Luke Dallas actually said please?

In one movement Luke was out of the chair, the tie holding his hands gone and his shirt shrugged off. He picked her off the floor and threw her on the bed. She landed on her back, stunned by the sudden change in elevation, her arms and legs akimbo. Before she could gather her thoughts as well as her limbs, she heard the rip of a foil packet.

Turning her head, she watched Luke roll the condom on with record speed before he joined her on the bed, removing all disappointment she hadn't been able to complete her task. He pulled the scrap of lace covering her entrance aside and then he was in her, his full length buried in her hot, needy depth.

She came so hard she saw galaxies of shooting stars,

their fiery trails matching the fire trailing in her veins, every nerve on full alert. Luke stilled above her and then he shouted her name, his full weight collapsing onto her. She didn't mind. She gathered him close to her, enjoying the raspy breathing in her ear, the scratch of his shaved cheek. For this brief minute, he was all hers.

Luke was spent. Completely, utterly, fully spent. He could feel his lungs working, so at least he was still alive. He didn't think his muscles would obey him even if the fate of the planet depended on it. But Danica was beneath him and he didn't want to crush her, so with a supreme effort he managed to roll to the side. She made a disappointed sound and followed him, curling against him.

That was…there were no words. Explosive, yes. Amazing, sure. But he'd had explosive, amazing sex before. He prided himself on ensuring both he and his partner left the bed with broad smiles on their faces. But all the superlatives in the world couldn't capture what he just experienced.

What he and Danica experienced together.

She stirred against him and he turned his head to see big green eyes blinking back at him. "Hey," she said with a small smile.

"Hey," he answered, and drew her into his arms. She sighed and put her head on his chest, her blond curls tangling in every direction. He tangled his fingers in them, loving the soft, springy texture. Her breathing deepened, became regular.

His limbs were heavy and he could feel himself following her into slumber, but he wanted to make the most of his time in her space. It afforded him a rare glimpse into the private Danica, which she kept so carefully guarded. Maybe that was why he reacted badly to the idea of some of her things remaining here. He wanted to have all of her.

The surface of her dresser was bare, except for a small collection of comic-book action figures. There was something in the way they stood, smiles on their faces, hands balled on their hips to take on the world, that reminded him of Danica. Her stance had been identical when she took on his parents.

On her nightstand, photos in silver frames showed Danica with an older man and woman he assumed were her parents. He frowned at the photo of a young man, handsome and confident in a football uniform. An old boyfriend? One she kept close to her pillow?

He must have moved, for Danica blinked awake. She looked up at him with a smile on her face, but it faded when she followed the direction of his gaze.

"That's my family," she said.

"I thought they were your parents. They look happy."

"They are." She paused. "Well, mostly."

"And the other photo?" He tried to sound casual.

She shifted away from him. He missed the tangle of her bare legs with his. "My brother. Matt."

"I didn't know you had siblings."

"Just the one. He's eight years younger. My mom said he was her best surprise ever. I think so too."

"You sound close."

"I was old enough to help with his care. Sometimes Matt jokes he doesn't have a sister, he has another mother."

He indicated the photo. "He plays football?"

She nodded. "He was a gifted athlete—basketball, baseball, soccer, you name it. But his true love was football."

"You said 'was.' He doesn't play now?"

"You caught that." She thinned her lips into a straight line, and then slowly released them. "Matt is a senior in high school. Colleges started to scout him during last season. Oh, not big programs like Stanford or USC. Smaller schools. His coaches told us if he played well this year, he might get a full scholarship. I can't tell you how much that would've meant to my parents." He caught the glint of tears in her eyes.

"What happened?"

She brushed the moisture away. "His helmet—we still don't know why, but it flew off when he took a big hit. He lost consciousness and when he woke up, he couldn't move his arms and legs. The doctors said he suffered partial cervical spinal-cord shock. It was a miracle he didn't break his neck."

"I'm sorry." He picked up the hand closest to him and held it tightly, hoping his grip would say what his words were too inadequate to convey.

She exhaled deeply. "The doctors don't believe the effects will be permanent. But he hasn't responded well to conventional treatment. And, obviously, the schools have stopped calling."

He pulled her to him, nestling her head against his chest. "Why didn't you say anything before this?"

He felt her shrug. "It's not anyone's business but ours," she said after minute. "Mine and my family's."

"I could've helped." His mind raced with avenues to explore, favors to call in. Medevco, the company Evan Fletcher and Grayson Monk pitched at Monte Carlo Night—weren't they involved in cutting-edge medical research? He was sure he'd read something about rehabilitating spinal-cord injuries in the prospectus they sent him.

She raised her head. "You have helped. Why do you think I accepted your job offer? We needed the money."

"I thought..." He stopped. The truth was his parents showed him everyone had a price. He thought he'd named hers. "I needed your skills, I made you an offer, you accepted. It's not a complicated equation."

She sat up and looked down at him. Golden curls hung in her face, begging him to twist them around his fingers and pull her face to his so he could kiss her senseless. Before he could suit action to thought, she gathered her tresses into a bun and tucked in the ends so it stayed put. "Your offer was preposterous."

Now it was his turn to sit up. "You said yes."

"Because I love my family and want to help them." Her gaze, which previously had been pinning his in place, dropped to the bedspread. "And, yes, now I can start my own executive search agency. But if we hadn't been desperate to pay for Matt's therapy, I wouldn't have jumped like I did."

Her sheets, which previously had felt silky smooth,

began to chafe. He couldn't find a comfortable spot. "It was a generous offer."

"I agree. And I appreciate being able to help my family. I owe you a lot."

"But you wouldn't have accepted otherwise." Not only were the sheets itchy, but the room was too hot. He pushed the covers down.

"No. I like taking bets, but finding you a wife? That would have been too professionally risky, even for me." She smiled at him, but it quickly turned into a frown. "You seem restless. Anything wrong?"

"No." Yes. Danica accepted his original offer only because of her family. Not for her own financial gain. It was counterintuitive to everything he knew to be true.

And he believed her. Her room spoke loudly of her affection for her family. Clusters of photo frames and mementos, cheap in price but cared for as if they belonged in the Louvre, told a clear story.

His carefully ordered world, already wobbling in its orbit, started to tilt. So, when Danica declared her love for him to his parents, did that mean…

No. It was a ploy. A feint in the bigger war. She said that only to win the battle.

Didn't she?

A shrill noise came from the direction of his discarded trousers, crumpled where they had been thrown. They both looked in that direction. "That's the ringtone for Anjuli," she said. "You should pick up."

He got out of bed and stalked to his pants. "Yes?"

"Check your texts," Anjuli said and hung up.

Frowning, he looked at his screen. Several texts

crowded the display. Nestor Stavros had unexpectedly returned to Palo Alto. He wanted to see Luke. Tomorrow.

He opened his mail app. His inbox was a jumble of new spreadsheets, press requests from his corporate communications team and questions about catering for the meeting. Too many details he had to get right. Now.

Danica cleared her throat. "What did Anjuli want?"

"I have to leave."

She blinked. "Right now?"

"Nestor Stavros came back to town early." He picked his shirt off the ground and buttoned it, then rebuttoned it when he realized he was off by a buttonhole. "He wants to meet in the morning."

She became very still. "The acquisition."

"Yes." He looked around for his socks. He found one by the door and the other under the bed.

She started to push back the covers. "Let me throw some clothes on and I'll go with you to the office."

"No need." He thrust his feet into his shoes and tied the laces, and then tried to give her a smile. He wasn't certain he succeeded. "Enjoy what's left of your time off."

Her gaze locked on his. "Are you okay?"

No. "Yes." Patting his pockets to make sure he had his wallet and keys, he straightened up and tried to give her a smile. It felt more like a grimace. "We'll know tomorrow if the marriage is a success."

"If the marriage is a—oh. Right." She sat back against the pillows. "So, do I say good luck, break a leg or…?"

"Let's hope for the best possible outcome." He

wanted to kiss her, but he was afraid it would cause him to stay with her for, oh, at least a week. Or whenever the food ran out. He settled for resting his lips against her forehead, allowing her scent to envelop him one more time before he left. "I'll drop the truck by the house and pick up my car before going to the office. It will probably be an all-nighter."

"Of course." She gave him a bright smile. "I might stay here, then, so I can see Mai when she gets home. One more girls' night."

There was a note in her voice he'd never heard before, but he shrugged it off as he hopped into his car. The prize he had been chasing for so long was in his grip. His employees could look forward to a very lucrative payout. Everyone would win.

But he couldn't help feeling he was missing a very big chunk of the game he was playing, and he'd left the clue to discovering it lying in a warm bed.

Ten

Danica walked the short distance from the train station to the Ruby Hawk offices, her gaze focused on the sidewalk. The weather had taken a chillier turn overnight, mimicking the cold descending on her heart when Luke exited the afternoon before.

She spent last night wide awake, trying to solve the mystery of why Luke had left so suddenly. Yes, he had to prepare for the meeting with Nestor, but something had been bothering him before he ran out of her home as if it were a condemned house. Had it been a mistake, allowing Luke into her private space, surrounded by her photos and mementos? Did it make him see the gap between them as insurmountable? There weren't a lot of ski medals and golf trophies hanging in display cases and littering her shelves after all. She pushed open the glass doors, barely hearing her coworkers' cheery hellos.

Maybe she'd revealed too much about her family? She didn't speak much about her brother or her parents' flight to the United States to escape a war determined to tear them apart. Her family long learned words of sympathy came quickly, but soon faded and disappeared—or even turned to annoyance—while problems lingered. So they stayed quiet and smiled as if they didn't have a care when asked, leaning only on each other.

Or maybe she was the problem. The few times she trusted someone enough to let them in, they left. Tom, her college boyfriend, hadn't wanted a partner whose family couldn't help support them. He'd discarded her for a fellow law student, whose biggest concern had been choosing which white-shoe firm to work for after graduation. Her former boss Johanna took off as soon as something shiny was dangled in front of her, heedless of the employee she knew was counting on the promotion. It was only par for the course, now that the acquisition was almost a reality, that Luke would be eager to finish this pretend marriage as soon as possible.

She pushed open the door to her tiny supply closet. Then she stopped short, her hand still on the doorknob. Her office was already occupied.

Irene Stavros leaned against a corner of Danica's desk, reading something tucked in a manila folder. "Hi!" she said with a cheerful smile. "I couldn't concentrate in the engineering bullpen, and my father is in Luke's office."

"Hi," Danica responded automatically. Irene looked spectacular. Her teal jersey dress clung in all the right spots, the color complementing her glowing olive complexion. If she wore any makeup to enhance her skin's flawlessness, Danica couldn't detect it. "Make yourself at home."

Irene beamed. "Thanks." She hopped off the desk and took the guest chair in front of Danica's desk. As soon as Danica sat down behind it, Irene began to speak. "I have so many things I need to discuss with you."

Danica switched on her computer, holding her sigh inside. Small talk with Irene was nowhere near her list of top ten things to do. "I'm all ears."

Irene clapped her hands and rubbed them together as if they were coconspirators. "Brilliant." She handed Danica the folder. "Let's start with what to say to the media."

Danica put it down on her desk without looking at it. "The corporate-communications department handles the press."

Irene shook her head, her shiny black tresses tossing as if they starred in a shampoo commercial. "We need to talk about Cinco Jackson and the story he is chasing." She raised an impeccably groomed eyebrow. "You're a big part of it."

The amorphous dread that had started to gather when Danica first spotted Irene coalesced into a hard, painful ball in Danica's stomach. "What story?"

Irene tapped the folder. "The one about Luke hiring you to be his wife to secure the acquisition, of course."

Luke greeted Nestor Stavros and ushered him to the conference table occupying the corner of Luke's office. "I hope you had a good flight?" he asked, taking the chair opposite him.

Nestor smiled and adjusted the cufflinks on his white linen French-cuff shirt. In contrast to Luke, who wore his usual work uniform of khaki trousers and a blue-checked button-down shirt, Nestor had on a fine wool Italian suit, custom tailored to make the heavily muscled man seem even more imposing. One would be hard pressed to tell Nestor had thirty years on Luke if it weren't for the liberal sprinkling of silver hairs at Nestor's temples and the deep creases at the corners of his dark eyes.

"Comfortable but long." His accent was a surprisingly harmonious combination of his native Greece and his adopted country, Australia. "It gave me time to review the documents. Impressive, the work you've accomplished."

"Good to hear." Luke leaned back in his chair. The welcome rush of adrenaline that accompanied a business negotiation hummed in his veins. The dance had begun, and they both knew the steps. "All is in order?"

"Mostly." Nestor did his own leaning. "Irene told me about your marriage. I am impressed. I didn't think you would go through with it."

"I met the right woman." Luke's words were glib. But as they left his mouth, he realized the truth. He did meet the right woman. Danica didn't have an Ivy League degree or come from generations of money. But she was...

Danica.

And that was all she needed to be.

The realization sank in, like a stone thrown into a lake. But the ripples it caused weren't upset or denial. On the contrary. For the first time in weeks he was supremely confident in his insight. Danica was his wife. The only wife he'd ever want.

But did she feel the same way? She didn't tell him about her brother even though he could have easily helped. Forget money. He had connections all over the world. He could have called in favors.

Nestor cleared his throat, snapping Luke's attention back to the meeting. "Lost in thoughts of your bride?" A knowing smirk appeared on Nestor's face. "It's just the two of us. You can drop the pretense."

"There's no pretense."

"You managed to fall in love and get married in such a hurry? You? A Dallas?" Nestor scoffed. "I admit I was reluctant to buy Ruby Hawk if you came with it. You come from a family that does not honor its obligations and is always chasing the next attractive...deal." He took a long sip of water from the glass in front of him, regarding Luke coolly over the rim. "My board begged me to walk away. But then Irene suggested the marriage clause. She said if you wanted the acquisition badly enough, you would find a way to make it happen, thus proving you have the drive and commitment we demand. Well done." He held out his hand to be shook.

Luke didn't take it. "The marriage clause was a ploy."

Nestor took his hand back with a small shrug. "I wouldn't say *ploy*. Think of it as the big battle before leveling up in a video game. After all, that's why we're acquiring Ruby Hawk. To enhance our interactive game technology." He took another sip. "Few have the persistence to make it this far. Much less get married just to secure the deal. That is the need to succeed at any cost I want in my people."

The air conditioning in his office must be set below freezing. That had to be why Luke's lips were numb and his fingers had lost all sensation.

"We have an agreement?" Nestor indicated the papers at Luke's elbow.

Bile started to rise. Luke pushed it down and drew the stack toward him. "Let me take a final look at the term sheet."

The offer was a good one. The stock his employees took in lieu of market-rate salaries would pay out at a rate beyond their wildest expectations. They deserved it for all their hard work. For placing their trust in him.

The hollow pit in his stomach grew into a yawning crater.

Nestor handed him a fountain pen, engraved with the date and location. "I had this made for the occasion." He chuckled. "To celebrate the marriage of our two companies."

Luke dropped the pen on hearing the word *marriage*. It rolled off the table and he leaned down to pick it up, but his fingers encountered something flat and circular instead. He pulled the item up, keeping his hand below the table.

It was a poker chip. A five-hundred-dollar poker chip. The one Danica handed to him at the Peninsula Society fund-raiser.

He stared. He'd been carrying it in his wallet ever since that night. It must have fallen out. A vision of Danica, her eyes sparkling as she watched the roulette wheel spin, danced before his eyes.

Nestor tapped the table. "There's champagne on rapidly melting ice."

Luke slipped the poker chip into his pocket, picking up his pen with his other hand. He sat up and pulled the stack of papers toward him. It really was an advantageous deal for Ruby Hawk Technologies, one that would ensure Luke's legacy would thrive and grow beyond what he could accomplish on his own.

His hand hesitated, the pen hovering over the paper.

Danica did her best to stop gaping like a fish yanked out of the water. "What? I don't—I mean…" She trailed off, still parsing Irene's words. She knew? How?

"I believe you wrote this." Irene took out a piece of paper and showed it to Danica.

It was a printout of her first contract with Luke. The one she created and sent via email the day they met. Danica froze.

"You remember Johanna?" Irene continued. "Of course, now Johanna works for the Stavros Group. When Cinco contacted her about the mysterious recruiter working for Luke Dallas who married him out of the blue, she was happy to look at the Rinaldi Executive Search files to see if there might be anything… untoward…we should know about." Irene indicated the contract. "That's what we found."

"This is a contract to act as a recruiter." Danica forced the words past her numb lips.

"Read the third paragraph. For a wife. In order to close the Stavros Group acquisition. And it seems one of your candidates was Cinco's fiancée. Bad luck, that."

Danica closed her eyes, but it didn't stop the horrifying visions playing before her. Luke's integrity questioned, her professional reputation destroyed beyond repair…her parents discovering her marriage had been a sham. "You can't blame Luke for trying to jump through the ridiculous hoops you set up—"

"Oh, I don't blame Luke for trying. Nicely done, by the way. Brava."

Apprehension prickled Danica's scalp. "What do you want, Irene?"

Irene smiled. It didn't reach her eyes. "Don't worry. I told Cinco I set you two up, and it was love at first sight. He'll find something else to write."

Irene killed the story? This wasn't a threat? "I don't understand."

"We're buying Ruby Hawk. We look after our own." Irene folded her hands on the desk. "And now you know that we know the truth. Consider it a favor saved in the bank. Just in case."

So it was a threat. "In case of what?"

Irene spread her hands wide. "Luke is happy to acquiesce to us now because of Ruby Hawk, but in the future?" She tapped the folder again. "We have insurance against any future rebellion. I don't need to tell you how much of a scandal we can spin this to be. But please, understand this isn't personal. I very much like you." She smiled, her even white teeth gleaming.

Danica didn't return it. She had to find Luke and warn him. If he signed the deal, he would be under the Stavros thumb. For good. "Anything else? I have work to do."

"Oh, yes, 'work.'" Irene made quote marks in the air with her fingers. "I am sorry, however, that you got dragged into this. You blindly walked into a game you didn't know you were playing. I blame Luke." She shrugged. "Desperate times, desperate measures."

The dry toast Danica choked down for breakfast threatened to make a reappearance. "I married Luke because I care for him."

Irene's smile turned into a smirk. "Of course. He's very attractive, especially in the bank account. And he knows how to use his words to get what he wants. But let's be honest. There's a reason why Luke and I aren't together. He is simply incapable of expressing any emotion that wasn't plotted on a spreadsheet. I'm sure you noticed that even in bed, he leaves after he gets what he wants. But well done on getting the diamond ring. At least you have something of tangible value in return."

Irene rose from Danica's desk. "Now that we're on the same page, my father wants to meet you. After all, as Luke's wife, you'll be spending quite a lot of time with us once Ruby Hawk becomes a Stavros Group subsidiary."

"You're wrong about Luke." Danica kept her chin raised. She wouldn't let Irene see how well her words hit her target. Luke was indeed good at using his words, and his other skills, to get what he wanted. And now that the acquisition was almost done... The memory of how he'd walked away from her bed, without a backward glance, played behind her eyelids.

"I'm wrong?" Irene tsked. "You're smarter than this." She stalked to the door, her long legs making short work of the distance from the desk. "We have a deal to celebrate. Coming?"

Danica could either get her heart rate under control or speak. She couldn't do both. She followed Irene in silence. At least now she had a chance to tell Luke about Nestor's and Irene's machinations, and he would find a way to get out of the deal. He wouldn't sell to the Stavros Group after hearing how they'd manipulated them both.

Would he?

Her heart wouldn't examine the answer too closely.

Luke looked up at the sound of the conference-room door opening, his pen still hovering above the signature page. Irene swept in, followed by... Danica? He sprung to his feet, a wide smile of welcome on his face. It disappeared as soon as he got a good look at her expression. It reminded him of the wide-eyed, stricken stare she gave him when they first met and she discovered Johanna had closed up shop without a word. "What's wrong?"

"What could possibly be wrong?" Irene arranged herself in a chair next to her father. "Shall I open the champagne?"

"When the deal memo has his signature." Nestor indicated the stack of paper.

Luke ignored them. He stepped to Danica's side and took her right hand in both of his. It felt like holding an ice cube. "Is everything okay?"

"You haven't signed?" Danica's gaze searched his.

"I'm about to. Why?"

She threw a glance at the Stavros father and daughter. "Can we speak? Alone?"

Irene took the foil off the neck of the champagne bottle. "She's about to tell you we know all about your fake marriage and we don't care."

Luke kept his gaze locked on Danica's as he responded to Irene. "Your father made it clear the marriage clause in the contract was fake, as well."

"The clause was a fake?" Danica's eyes widened. "But of course it was. Just another move in the game."

"It worked." Irene shrugged. "Better than we ever could have anticipated. We alleviated our board's concerns about Luke's stability, we own Ruby Hawk, and, thanks to both of you, we have leverage for the future. Oh, that's the other thing she wants to tell you, Luke. We have written proof of your marriage scam." She popped the champagne cork. "Useful, that. Someday, I'm sure."

Nestor looked at his diamond-encrusted Rolex.

"Can we get back to business? I leave for Los Angeles in a half hour to meet with my bankers. If we don't have an agreement today, it will be months before the board will approve another offer." He raised an eyebrow. "I've seen your financials, my boy. You don't have months left."

Danica turned to Luke, her hand still locked in his. "You can't sell. Not to them." Her gaze pleaded with him.

"Come with me." Luke ushered her out of the conference room to a small alcove nearby where they could speak somewhat privately. But anyone could walk by, and he was aware they were drawing curious glances from the engineers sitting in the open plan bullpen. He lowered his voice. "I'm signing the deal. I have to. It will ensure Ruby Hawk's future."

Danica's already pale complexion turned ghostly white. "But you heard what they said. You'll never be free of them. You're selling yourself out."

"It's going to be okay." He wanted to push an errant curl behind her ear. He settled for a tight smile. "This won't change anything between us."

She pulled her hand away from his, her head shaking. "You mean you're okay. I'm not. They admit they have the game rigged but you're still playing." She hugged her arms close, her shoulders hunched. "And things *will* change. Our marriage ends when the acquisition is a done deal. Not that we had to get married in the first place, apparently."

The mention of their agreement caused his gut to

contract. "It doesn't need to end. We'll find a way to negate any leverage Irene thinks she has."

Her gaze locked on his. "There you go, changing the strategy again. Don't you understand? This isn't about our agreement. It's about you and the Stavroses. If you take the deal, the game continues. But you can stop it, now, by saying no to them. If you don't—" she took a deep breath "—I will. I will walk away. I won't be a threat held over your head."

"I'll handle it. You just need to trust me."

Danica's head jerked back. "Trust you? Tell me why, Luke. Why should I trust you?"

He was missing something. Something very important. But he didn't have time to puzzle it out. "Because I have everything under control."

"That's what you tell business colleagues. Tell *me* why I should trust you." Her gaze pleaded with him.

"I…" In the corner of his peripheral vision, Irene emerged from the conference room and tapped her watch in his direction. "We'll straighten this out after Nestor leaves. We need to get back to the meeting."

It was the wrong thing to say. He knew it even as the words left his mouth and hung in the air between them.

This should have been a day of triumph. He'd ensured the future growth of Ruby Hawk. His employees would be financially rewarded for all their hard work. But Danica's stunned expression, her eyes wide and suspiciously bright, told him he'd just lost more than he could imagine.

"There's nothing I can say to stop you from this, is there?" She played with her hands. It took him a moment to realize what she was doing. By then, her wedding rings were off her finger and lying on her outstretched right palm. "Here. At least they won't be able to use me against you."

No. This wasn't what he wanted. A bone-chilling freeze rooted him in place.

"Take them. Once the acquisition is done and our marriage is over, they'd be returned to you anyway," she continued. When he didn't move, couldn't move, she picked up his right hand. Her touch burned as they placed the rings in his grasp and closed his nerveless fingers around them.

He got his lips to function. "Danica...don't... I need..."

"No. You don't need me. Turns out you never needed me." She looked over his shoulder, and her gaze sharpened. "Irene is heading our way."

He couldn't get a grip on his panicked thoughts. They bounced and tangled around his skull, refusing to be sorted. "This isn't—"

"Congratulations on the deal. I mean that. Goodbye, Luke." She kissed his cheek, her lips hot against his chilled skin, and turned on her heels. She was through the nearest exit before he could get his feet to move.

Irene put her hand on his forearm, pulling him back when he would follow Danica. Irene's touch reminded him he still stood in the middle of the engineering bullpen. It was more crowded than normal. He recognized people from sales, accounting and marketing, attempting to appear as if they were busy and not eavesdropping.

"Can we sign now?" Irene asked.

He didn't answer, his gaze locked on the rings in his hand, his brain trying to process the image. Every atom in his being urged him to go after Danica. His employees' sideways glances reminded him he was minutes away from securing their futures. A headache gathered behind his eyes. The pain dulled his senses while sharpening his regret.

Irene glanced down at the jewelry. "Too bad. I was honest when I said I liked her."

Her words cut through the aching fog shutting him down. "What else did you say to her?"

She scoffed. "Don't blame your inability to maintain a relationship on me."

"What did you say?" He enunciated each word.

Her gaze widened, and for a second something like hurt entered her gaze. Then she blinked, and her smooth mask of amused indifference was back in place. "Such emotion in your voice," she said lightly. "One might think you have a heart after all."

He didn't react, his gaze continuing to pin her in place.

"We had a discussion about your ability to stay unaffected when it came to affairs of the bed," she said, with an airy gesture of her hand. "Girl talk."

"Danica agreed?" That sliced through the numbness, a full body slam of hurt.

Irene rolled her eyes. "She defended you. Which is why it's for the best she left. If she stayed, she'd be devoured and spit out in less than a year."

Luke stopped listening after the first three words.

Danica defended him. She must care. But if she did, why did she leave? Why wouldn't she trust—

When there's no caring, there can't be trust. Her words rang in his head.

He put a hand on the wall to steady himself. Of course. That was the piece he was missing, the clue he couldn't see. She couldn't trust him because he hadn't shown her he could be trusted with her heart. She didn't know how much—

"I love her."

He wasn't aware he did until he said the words out loud. Now he couldn't fathom how he hadn't known. How could he not? He knew how he reacted to her. How his heart rate sped up when he saw her name on his phone's caller ID. How a brush of her fingers against his was enough to arouse him, deep and heavy. How his knees turned to water when she took her hair down and shook the curls free.

He wanted her voice to be the last thing he heard at night. Her face the first thing he saw in the morning. To laugh and argue and sit in companionable silence after stuffing themselves too full during Sunday brunch. The thought of a toddler with golden ringlets took his breath away.

In the past, he might have cataloged these as mere physiological reactions to mental stimuli and nothing more. Even an hour ago, before the meeting with Nestor, he might have argued with himself not to allow intangible feelings to distract him from solid goals.

Now there was only one goal that mattered. He

glimpsed a life without Danica and it was a dark and dreary place indeed.

He wasn't his parents. He wasn't his family and their interminable feuds. He could forge his own path, one of love and laughter and growing old with the grandmother of the babies crawling at their feet.

One of trust and commitment.

He strode to the conference room, leaving Irene in his wake. He signed the deal memo below Nestor's thick scrawl, and made sure his lawyers had their copies before Nestor left for his flight to Los Angeles. Then he called Anjuli into his office.

He knew what he had to do.

Eleven

Danica descended the stairs of her parents' home and found her mother seated at the kitchen table. Amila Novak smiled a warm greeting at her, but her expression quickly turned puzzled. "I'm happy you put on a fresh shirt to visit Matt, but why do you need a suitcase?"

The handle of her carry-on bag in one hand, Danica held out her phone, the browser opened to the *Silicon Valley Weekly* website, with the other. "The Ruby Hawk board of directors approved the sale to the Stavros Group. But Luke is no longer the CEO. That wasn't the plan. Something went wrong."

Amila put down her coffee cup. "So you're what… going to California? Now?"

"I have to explain. Get him reinstated somehow. Running Ruby Hawk is all he ever wanted."

"I thought you left precisely because all he wanted was his company." Her mom leaned forward, her chin cupped in her hand. "But I'm glad to see your eyes so alive again. When you showed up here out of the blue, it seemed nothing would get you out of your bed except visiting Matt."

Danica dropped her gaze. When she boarded the plane in San Francisco, she had no intention of ever seeing Luke again. But then Mai called to say that Luke returned all of Danica's things, in person, ensuring everything went back exactly the way she had it. Then he bought Mai dinner as an apology for invading her home—and donated fifty thousand dollars to Mai's pediatric unit at the hospital. He was still an ass though, she was quick to add in female solidarity.

Aisha texted her when she ran into Luke at a local grocery store over the weekend. That was a shock in itself as Luke usually had all his food delivered. Aisha reported he was wandering the aisles, almost as if he was there just to get out of his house.

He came up to me as soon as we locked eyes to ask about you. He still had that hungry look, and it wasn't for anything on the shelves.

Luke did call Danica a few times. She let the calls go to voice mail but sent him a text with her parents' address, so his lawyers would know where to send the divorce papers. A clean break was the best for all concerned, she lied to herself. But ghosting him added to her current remorse. What if he'd needed her to be present for the Ruby Hawk sale? She wouldn't put it past Nestor or Irene to pull a last-minute clause out of their bag of dirty tricks. The guilt of costing him the deal would eat her alive.

She raised her gaze to meet her mother's. "All I know is if I can set things right for him, then I need to do it." She picked up her bag. "If I leave now, I might make the next flight."

"Wait." Amila sprung to her feet. "You can't leave now. What about—" She coughed suddenly. "What about Matt? You're going to leave without saying good-bye to Matt?"

"I need to do this. Matt knows I love him." Danica moved toward the kitchen door. "I'll be back before you know it."

Her mother grabbed the handle of the suitcase and wouldn't let go. "If you want to leave after seeing your brother, fine. But you must come with us. Look, here's your father now." She nodded at the man coming down the stairs.

"Is everyone ready?" Mirko Novak grabbed the car keys off the table before taking his first look at Danica. "A clean shirt like we asked. Well done."

"She thinks she's going to the airport. To go to California," Amila told her husband.

Mirko's gaze widened. "She can't go. She needs to see—" He stopped, and cleared his throat. "Matt," he finished, sounding slightly…panicked? *But why would he be panicked?* She must be imagining things.

Amila nodded. "That's what I said."

Danica's gaze ping-ponged between her parents.

"What's going on? Why is seeing Matt today so important?"

"Visiting your brother is not important?" Mirko raised his dark eyebrows. He took her by the elbow and steered her toward the garage and the car parked inside over her protests. "Tell me more about California while I drive."

"Fine," she grumbled and put on her seat belt. She would go to the airport that afternoon and find another flight. A few more hours wouldn't hurt. Or so she crossed her fingers.

When they arrived at the center, Danica signed in and then turned left at the reception desk to go to her brother's room. Her mother caught her arm. "Matt's doctor wants to see us first, alone."

Danica frowned. "Is everything okay?"

"He wants to go over a new treatment with us, as the parents." Amila shrugged. "You know doctors."

"Uh-huh." Danica narrowed her gaze. First, they insisted she had to see Matt. Now they insisted she not see him? "I'll wait here. For a little bit."

Her mom squeezed her hand. "Thanks, *draga*."

Her parents disappeared through the automatic glass double doors that led to the residential wing, leaving Danica with the security guard for company. Still, it wasn't an unpleasant place to wait. Sunshine streamed in through floor-to-ceiling windows, while comfortable-looking white chairs invited her to sit down. The clean, modern decor reminded her of the Ruby Hawk offices. Which reminded her of Luke. But then most things did.

That man coming through the glass doors, for example, was a dead ringer for—

The world stopped spinning. Then it spun too fast. He wasn't a ringer for Luke.

He *was* Luke.

She could only watch, her feet rooted to the ground, as he made his way to her. "Hi," he said, stopping in front of her.

"Hi," she squeaked. So many questions ran through her head, she didn't know which ones to articulate. She settled for staring at him.

He looked good. So good. His dark hair was a smidge longer and as windswept as ever. His blue eyes sparkled like the Pacific Ocean on a calm summer's day. The crisp white shirt he wore was unbuttoned at the top. She took a step closer, to see if he still smelled the same, but jumped back when she realized what she was doing. Then she frowned. His trousers had a shiny stripe running down their outer legs.

"Why are you wearing tuxedo pants?" It wasn't the most brilliant question with which to start. But his face creased into a wide smile. He put both hands in his pockets and came up with two closed fists.

"Because I was wearing them when you gave me this." He opened his left hand. On his palm was a five hundred-dollar poker chip.

The room wouldn't stop revolving. "You flew across the country to return it?"

"No." His fingers closed over the chip before she could pluck it from his grasp. "I came here to ask you to take another risk."

Her heart, which had been beating a hopeful symphony, settled into a more sedate melody. She had been right. He needed her, but to get his company back. "I read about the board of directors removing you as CEO. If it's because I left before the deal closed, I'm happy to speak to whomever—"

"No." He shook his head.

"No?" It was worse than she thought. "But they can't take Ruby Hawk from you! The company means everything to you."

"There is only one thing that means everything to me. And that's my wife." He opened his right fist.

Her wedding ring sat on his palm, shining like a blazing star, sending refracted shards of rainbow dancing around the room.

She stared at it, caught between holding her breath and hyperventilating, as he held it out. "The board of directors didn't remove me. I resigned. Anjuli is the new CEO. She's more than a match for Nestor," he said.

His blue gaze was alight with so much emotion it made her tremble. "I don't understand. You gave up Ruby Hawk?"

"You were right. I had to stop the game. Stop allowing the past to dictate the future. Stop controlling the present." He smiled, and it was so tender her breath caught. "Allow for serendipity."

Hope started to flower, big, showy blossoms of delight and joy. Her veins sang with it. "What about Irene? And my email about our contract? Cinco Jackson's exposé?"

He laughed. "I called Cinco and told him the whole

thing." He held up the hand with the chip again. "Took a risk, but it paid off. He was much more intrigued about the Stavros Group hacking email to find blackmail material on their potential business partners than he was in our contract. Irene is busy fending off his phone calls."

The grin on her face painfully stretched her skin, but she didn't care. "So you're not going to start a new company and sell it under ridiculous conditions?"

"A new company, yes. I've already talked to Grayson Monk and Evan Fletcher about joining Medevco. But no more conditions." He stepped closer, his scent teasing her nose. She yearned to throw her arms around his neck and press her lips to the skin just below his jaw, inhaling more of it, for the rest of time. "I'm never letting you go again. I love you, Danica Novak."

It was a good thing she was in a medical facility, because she wasn't sure her heart could hold all the happiness. She cupped his beloved face with her hands, tracing the faint lines that appeared in his forehead, reveling in the prickle of his five-o'clock shadow against her fingertips.

"You didn't shave this morning," she babbled, scarcely aware she spoke as she bathed in the heat and passion and love—yes, love—radiating from his gaze.

"I was in too much of a hurry to do this." And then his mouth was on hers and she couldn't think at all, lost in the wonder that was Luke kissing her, reaffirming just how much she meant to him. She melted into him, her lips opening under his, pressing as close to him as the thin barrier of their clothes would allow. She—

Someone tapped on her shoulder. Through the heat and haze, a voice said, "Hey, I hate to break this up, but..."

It sounded like Matt. But he should be in his room.

Danica disengaged from Luke and turned to whoever interrupted them. And then she clung to Luke even harder.

It *was* Matt. And Matt—Matt was standing. As she stared, blinking, he grinned and began to walk.

Oh, he was holding onto a walker, and his progress was slow. But he was moving his legs.

"Look at you." Tears, which had been threatening to form ever since she first spotted Luke, now leaked down her cheeks. Luke handed her a packet of tissues, which she gratefully accepted. Then she frowned at her brother. "Have you been hiding your progress from me?"

"Just this past week. Got access to some new therapies," he said, nodding at Luke.

"From Luke?" She gaped at him.

Luke smiled and tucked her against his side. "It was your idea to use Ruby Hawk technology in sports equipment that got me started. Medevco's products include revolutionary tools for use in physical therapy. Matt was kind enough to be one of our test subjects."

The tears burned hot on her cheeks. But then, joy should feel warm. "Thank you for helping my brother."

"He's family," Luke said simply.

Danica's gaze searched his face. Once upon a time she thought he resembled a brooding man of the moors, solitary, disdaining help from other people. And he still did—but the aura of utter self-sufficiency was no longer evident. "Family isn't a four-letter word now?"

"My parents are who they are. But love is a four-letter word too. And speaking of…" He turned to face her. Then he dropped to one knee.

She didn't think the day could hold any more shocks. Luke Dallas didn't stoop to others. Luke Dallas walked on top of them. But there he was. Kneeling. In front of her. "What are you doing?" She forced the words past lips numb with surprise and hope.

"What I should have done the first time." He took her hands in his, his grip warm and firm and oh so right. "When you left, you took the sun with you. I want you to come back. Be my light. Be my wife."

Her heart expanded, shutting out doubts and fears with a strength beyond measure. "I love you too," she said, her voice shaking. "I have ever since we kissed outside the taqueria."

He pressed his lips against her left palm. Then he slid the diamond and platinum band on the ring finger. "Will you do me the honor of remaining my wife?"

"Yes. Yes!" And then his mouth was on hers. She gladly opened to him, winding her arms around his neck and pressing closer. She hadn't known just how deeply she missed him until she could smell and taste and touch him once again.

"Hey, guys? People are waiting for the main event," she heard her brother say. Luke laughed and lifted his head, keeping a tight arm around her waist.

"What main event? What could possibly come next?" Her gaze locked on Luke's. She would never grow tired of watching the light dance in those summer-sea depths.

Luke smiled. "You said our last wedding wasn't a real one because your family wasn't there. So…" He took his phone out of his pocket and pushed a button on the screen. The opening chords of "My Shot" from *Hamilton* filled the air. "Your mother has a dress waiting for you. I'll meet you in the center's chapel when you're ready."

She didn't know so much happiness existed in the world. "We're already married." She held up her decorated ring finger. "Another ceremony wouldn't be practical."

He growled, causing her to laugh. "I'm learning to let go when it comes to control, but I'm not letting you go ever again. I'll marry you a hundred times. You can plan the next wedding."

"Just twice will do," she said. "As long as the contract term is forever."

"At least that long," he warned. "Trust me."

Danica smiled. They weren't in the chapel yet, but it was a vow to him that was long overdue. "I do. Forever."

* * * * *

COMING NEXT MONTH FROM

⟨H⟩ HARLEQUIN®
Desire

Available June 4, 2019

#2665 HIS TO CLAIM
The Westmoreland Legacy • by Brenda Jackson
Honorary Westmoreland Thurston "Mac" McRoy delayed a romantic ranch vacation with his wife for too long—she went without him! Now it will take all his skills to rekindle their desire and win back his wife...

#2666 RANCHER IN HER BED
Texas Cattleman's Club: Houston • by Joanne Rock
Rich rancher Xander Currin isn't looking for a relationship. Cowgirl Frankie Walsh won't settle for anything less. When combustible desire consumes them both just as secrets from Frankie's past come to light, will their passion survive?

#2667 TAKEN BY STORM
Dynasties: Secrets of the A-List • by Cat Schield
Isabel Withers knows her boss, hotel executive Shane Adams, should be off-limits—but the chances he'll notice her are zilch. Until they're stranded together in a storm and let passion rule. Can their forbidden love overcome the scandals waiting for them?

#2668 THE BILLIONAIRE'S BARGAIN
Blackout Billionaires • by Naima Simone
Chicago billionaire Darius King never surrenders...until a blackout traps him with an irresistible beauty. Then the light reveals his enemy—his late best friend's widow! Marriage is the only way to protect his friend's legacy, but soon her secrets will force Darius to question everything...

#2669 FROM MISTAKE TO MILLIONS
Switched! • by Andrea Laurence
A DNA kit just proved Jade Nolan is *not* a Nolan. Desperate for answers, she accepts the help of old flame Harley Dalton—even though she knows she can't resist him. What will happen when temptation leads to passion and the truth complicates everything?

#2670 STAR-CROSSED SCANDAL
Plunder Cove • by Kimberley Troutte
When Chloe Harper left Hollywood to reunite with her family, she vowed to heal herself before hooking up with *anyone*. But now sexy star-maker Nicolas Medeiros is at her resort, offering her the night of her dreams. She takes it...and more. But how will she let him go?

YOU CAN FIND MORE INFORMATION ON UPCOMING HARLEQUIN® TITLES, FREE EXCERPTS AND MORE AT WWW.HARLEQUIN.COM.

HDCNM0519

SPECIAL EXCERPT FROM

HQN™

*Beatrix Leighton has loved Gold Valley cowboy
Dane Parker from afar for years, and she's about to
discover that forbidden love might just be the sweetest...*

Read on for a sneak preview of
Unbroken Cowboy
by New York Times *and* USA TODAY
bestselling author Maisey Yates.

It was her first kiss. But that didn't matter.

It was Dane. That was all that mattered. That was all that really mattered.

Dane, the man she'd fantasized about a hundred times—maybe a thousand times—doing this very thing. But this was so much brighter and more vivid than a fantasy could ever be. Color and texture and taste. The rough whiskers on his face, the heat of his breath, the way those big, sure hands cupped her face as his lips moved slowly over hers.

She took a step and the shattered glass crunched beneath her feet, but she didn't care. She didn't care at all. She wanted to breathe in this moment for as long as she could, broken glass be damned. To exist just like this, with his lips against hers, for as long as she possibly could.

She leaned forward, wrapped her fingers around the fabric of his T-shirt and clung to him, holding them both steady, because she was afraid she might fall if she didn't.

Her knees were weak. Like in a book or a movie.

She hadn't known that kissing could really, literally, make your knees weak. Or that touching a man you wanted could make you feel like you were burning up, like you had a fever. Could make you feel hollow and restless and desperate for what came next...

Even if what came next scared her a little.

It was Dane.

She trusted Dane.

With her secrets. With her body.

Dane.

She breathed his name on a whispered sigh as she moved to take their kiss deeper, and found herself being set back, glass crunching beneath her feet yet again.

"I should go," he said, his voice rough.

"No!" The denial burst out of her, and she found herself reaching forward to grab his shirt again. "No," she said again, this time a little less crazy and desperate.

She didn't feel any less crazy and desperate.

"I have to go, Bea."

"You don't. You could stay."

The look he gave her burned her down to the soles of her feet. "I can't."

"If you're worried about… I didn't misunderstand. I mean I know that if you stayed we would…"

"Dammit, Bea," he bit out. "We can't. You know that."

"Why? I'm not stupid. I know you don't want… I don't want…" She stumbled over her words because it all seemed stupid. To say something as inane as she knew they wouldn't get married. Even saying it made her feel like a silly virgin.

She was a virgin. There wasn't really any glossing over that. But she didn't have to seem silly.

She did know, though. For all that everyone saw her as soft and naive, she wasn't. She'd carried a torch for Dane for a long time but she'd also realistically seen how marriage worked. Her brother was a cheater. Her mother was a cheater.

Her father was… She didn't even know.

That was the legacy of love and marriage in her family.

Truly, she didn't want any part of it.

Some companionship, though. Sex. She wanted that. With him. Why couldn't she have that? McKenna made it sound simple, and possible. And Bea wanted it.

Don't miss
Unbroken Cowboy *by Maisey Yates,*
available May 2019 wherever Harlequin® books
and ebooks are sold.

www.Harlequin.com

*Honorary Westmoreland Thurston "Mac" McRoy
delayed a romantic ranch vacation with his wife for too
long—she went without him! Now it will take all his
skills to rekindle their desire and win back his wife...*

Read on for a sneak peek at
His to Claim
by New York Times *bestselling author Brenda Jackson!*

Thurston McRoy, called Mac by all who knew him, still had
his arms around his mother's shoulders when he felt her tense
up. "Mom? You okay?" he asked, looking down at her.

When his parents glanced over at each other, that uneasy
feeling from earlier crept over him again. Not liking it, he
turned to go down the hall toward his bedroom when his father
reached out to stop him.

"Teri isn't here, Mac."

Mac turned back to his father. His mother had moved to
stand beside his dad.

"It's after two in the morning and tomorrow is a school day
for the girls. So where is she?"

His mother reached out and touched his arm. "She needed
to get away and she asked if we would come keep the girls."

Mac frowned. He knew his wife. She would not have gone
anywhere without their daughters. "What do you mean, she
needed to get away? Why?"

"She's the one who has to tell you that, Thurston. It's not
for us to say."

Mac drew in a deep breath, not understanding any of this. Because his parents were acting so secretive, he felt his confusion and anger escalating. "Fine. Where is she?"

It was his father who spoke. "She left three days ago for the Torchlight Dude Ranch."

Mac's frown deepened. "The Torchlight Dude Ranch? In Wyoming?"

"Yes."

"What the hell did she go there for?"

His father didn't say anything for a minute and then gave Mac an answer. "She said she always wanted to go back there."

Mac rubbed his hand across his face. Yes, Teri had always wanted to go back there, the place he'd taken her on their honeymoon, a little over ten years ago. And he'd always promised to take her back. But between his covert missions and their growing family, there had never been enough time. Teri, who'd been raised on a ranch in Texas, was a cowgirl at heart and had once dreamed of being on the rodeo circuit due to her roping and riding skills. She'd even represented the state of Texas as a rodeo queen years ago.

When they'd married, she had given it all up to travel around the world with her naval husband. She'd said she'd done so gladly. Why in the world would Teri leave their kids and go to a dude ranch by herself?

He knew the only person who could answer that question was Teri.

It was time to go find his wife.

His to Claim

by New York Times *bestselling author Brenda Jackson,
available June 2019 wherever
Harlequin® Desire books and ebooks are sold.*

www.Harlequin.com

Copyright © 2019 by Brenda Streater Jackson

HDEXP0519

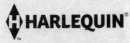

Love Harlequin romance?

DISCOVER.

Be the first to find out about promotions, news and exclusive content!

Facebook.com/HarlequinBooks

Twitter.com/HarlequinBooks

Instagram.com/HarlequinBooks

Pinterest.com/HarlequinBooks

ReaderService.com

EXPLORE.

Sign up for the Harlequin e-newsletter and download a free book from any series at **TryHarlequin.com.**

CONNECT.

Join our Harlequin community to share your thoughts and connect with other romance readers!
Facebook.com/groups/HarlequinConnection

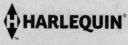

HARLEQUIN®

**ROMANCE WHEN
YOU NEED IT**

HSOCIAL2018